Charles Gibbon

Robin Gray

A novel. Part 3

Charles Gibbon

Robin Gray
A novel. Part 3

ISBN/EAN: 9783337065836

Printed in Europe, USA, Canada, Australia, Japan

Cover: Foto ©Andreas Hilbeck / pixelio.de·

More available books at **www.hansebooks.com**

BY

CHARLES GIBBON

AUTHOR OF "DANGEROUS CONNEXIONS."

*

" Had we never loved sae kindly,
Had we never loved sae blindly,
Never met—or never parted,
We had ne'er been broken-hearted."
—*Burns*

IN THREE VOLUMES.

VOL. III.

LONDON:
BLACKIE & SON, PATERNOSTER ROW;
AND GLASGOW AND EDINBURGH.
1869.

GLASGOW:

W. G. BLACKIE AND CO., PRINTERS,

VILLAFIELD

CONTENTS.

VOLUME III.

ROBIN GRAY.

CHAPTER I.

ON THE SEA.

"The white waves heaving high, my lads,
The good ship tight and free—
The world of waters is our home,
And merry men are we."—*Allan Cunningham.*

ONE feels the loss of a nearly won victory more bitterly than a hundred defeats in which the tide has been contrary from the start. Jeanie had been so near success this night, had been so near the complete solution of the mystery which surrounded James Falcon's death, that the disappointment of her failure scourged her with sharper pangs than even the dread of what was to become of her could do.

True she had heard no confession, no refer-

ence to the event which might not have been
easily explained as referring to something
else.   But she had heard and seen enough to
prove that the Laird and Carrach were at the
bottom of it all.   The former had threatened
his companion with the gallows, and he had
warned him that Mr. Carnegie was inquiring
after him.   For what other reason could he
have done this than the one she assigned for
it—their complicity in the crime? That document which the Laird had caused the skipper
to sign, that he might hold it as a threat
over him, she felt satisfied contained all the
information requisite to release her husband.

And yet here she was, out at sea, a helpless
prisoner in the hands of the man whose life
was at stake.   Here she was unable to stir
hand or foot, with the waters rapidly deepen-
ing between her and any chance of rescue.
She had been too much accustomed to the
sea from her babyhood up to be disturbed by
it now, although the little boat was tossed
by the waves with perilous violence.

But what was this dull brute at whose

mercy she was placed going to do with her? She had heard him say that he was to take her with him. Did he mean that, or was he only carrying her out to sea that it might close over another crime? He could trust the deep ocean to keep his secret. She shuddered at the thought, and yet oddly as it appeared to herself at the time, she did not feel so much afraid as she had done at first when struggling with him on land. The utter desperation of her position seemed to endue her with calmness and fortitude which surprised herself.

He did not speak; she did not move; and she caught herself counting the dips of the oars with a dull mechanical fidelity, as if she were to calculate by the number of strokes the distance which was being placed between her and safety and all that was most precious to her.

A black mass rose above the water, at first like a cloud, but soon assuming the proportions of a schooner.

The Highlander suddenly ceased rowing,

shipped his oars, and bent toward her. She shrunk within herself with constrained breath as he touched her. But the fear which affected her was dispelled immediately. Instead of heaving her out of the boat as she had thought he purposed doing, he unfastened her hands, and removed the gag from her mouth.

"You'll no care to jump into the water," he said; "and if you'll do—I'll no care. So you can hae the use o' your arms and feet now."

He took the oars again and pulled to the side of the schooner. He hallooed to those on board, and a man looked over the bulwark.

"Wha's that?" said the man, as if somebody had knocked at the door.

"Shust me and my guidwife, Donald," responded the skipper; "gie's a hand."

Donald assisted Carrach to convey Jeanie on deck by means of a rope-ladder. She did not make any objection or speak a word of any kind. She obeyed the directions given her quietly and silently. Words could not help her now; cries and lamentations would be worse than useless. All she could do was to submit, and observe every movement of those about for any chance of escape.

She noted particularly, and it was the first gleam of hope she obtained, that the small boat was not hauled up: it was permitted to float astern.

Carrach asked her to descend to the cabin, where she could go to sleep if she liked. She spoke for the first time since they had left shore, and asked him to let her remain on deck. He seemed to be peculiarly willing to humour her, and consented: "it was all the same one thing to him—would she hae a dram?"

"No."

"Very goot, he would hae one himself, and his lads would hae one, and they would all drink her goot health and a pleasant voyage."

He rolled down to his cabin, and before he returned Donald's comrade appeared from the forecastle, where he had been sleeping. Of these two men Jeanie was unable to form any opinion, as there was not light enough for her to see their faces distinctly, and to read there what hope she might have of enlisting their sympathies on her behalf. So far they were nothing more than two dark figures lounging about the deck in the dim light, utterly indifferent to her presence, or how she had come to be there.

The skipper returned with a bottle, gave each of his men a dram, and took a double one himself.

Two things she observed: the double dram, and the fact that he had left below the canvas-bag he had obtained from the Laird. She had seen him take it down with him, and she wondered if that canvas-bag could help her in her strait. It was a strange thought, quite without shape as yet; but her mind was painfully alert, watching everything.

By the united effort of the three men the anchor was raised, the foresails were set, and the vessel began slowly to move seaward.

When she became sensible of the motion of the schooner, Jeanie experienced a sharp pang at her heart; and she turned her eyes wistfully toward the shore, which melted like a black line into the sky. She was being borne away she did not know whither by a man who had the strongest possible motive for keeping her safe prisoner. She might never see that shore again; or, worse, she might return to it too late to serve the husband for whose sake she had risked so much.

A dreary, hopeless, sickening sensation oppressed her, and she clutched the bulwark by which she was standing to keep herself from falling. The skipper's voice roused her. He was giving some directions to the man who had come up from the forecastle, and whose name she caught—Grainger.

She turned as she heard him mutter some surly response about over-work and the obligation to do double duty in consequence of there not being a proper number of hands on board. He moved aft to the helm.

Here was another straw to catch at: there were only three men on board. She remembered now Carrach mentioning that to the

Laird. They must sleep sometime ; perhaps only one would be left on deck. Then it would be possible to elude him and to slip over the side into the small boat. Once in it, with a fair start and the night to help her, she had no fear of making her escape. Thanks to the fact that she was a fisherman's daughter, she knew how to handle an oar, and she was devoid of all squeamish feeling regarding the water.

Her pulse quickened with hope as she speculated on this prospect. She was not going to despair yet, or lose precious opportunity in useless fretting. She had a sacred object to achieve, and at that thought the resolution with which she had tracked the Laird again obtained sway over her. She would be cool and watchful as a tiger preparing to spring on its prey, ready to snatch at the first chance which presented itself.

Her ardour was slightly damped, however, when Carrach approached her and bade her a second time go down to the cabin.

"Can ye no let me bide here?" she said

quietly. "I canna walk on the water, so ye canna be feared that I'll win awa'."

"Oich no, I'll no be feared of that at all, or I would no hae left you here this long time; and you'll no care to droon yoursel', as I'll thocht before; and I'll no care if you do, as I'll thocht before too. So you can bide here if you'll like it, and you'll go below in the daylight and sleep when I'll no want you to be seen on deck."

His rough manner again showed a desire to please her in complying with her request, and his eyes rolled with as near an approach to an expression of satisfaction as they were capable of expressing anything.

She did not like the idea; but she had resolved to lose no chance of gaining her object, and in spite of the loathing which his person and the conviction of his crime inspired, she would not cast away the opportunity which this idea promised: if she could satisfy him that she was hopeless of escape, and resigned to her position on board the schooner, half her difficulty would be overcome. She might even carry away with her some proof which would enable her to force a full confession from the Laird. She was already thinking of what was to be done when she reached Portlappoch again, and without that confession she feared that it would be impossible to obtain credence for the wild story she would have to tell of this night's work.

She was still leaning on the bulwark, her face turned shoreward, but observing him with quick furtive glances.

He was standing within arm's reach of her, stolid and heavy as if he had become fixed to the deck, his eyes rolling slowly over her from head to foot.

"Where are ye taking me to now?" she said, controlling an impulse to shrink away from him.

"Wherever we go."

"Where are ye going to then?"

"I'll not know right yet—the first port we can get hands at."

"Will ye let me out there?"

"No, we couldna do that. You'll go with us."

"What for—what harm do ye fear frae me?"

"I'll not know what harm, and that's shust what for I'll took you wi' me. While I see you here, I'll know it was all right; but when I'll no see you nowhere, I'll not know but it's all wrong."

Slow as he might be in grasping an idea, he held fast to it when he had got it, and he had all the cunning instinct of the brute creation where his own safety was concerned. He had shown that in his dealings with the Laird; and he showed it now in dealing with his prisoner, notwithstanding the desire he manifested to humour her.

"Do ye mean that ye're gaun to keep me here ay?"

"Shust that."

"Oh, man, what guid will it do ye to keep me awa' frae my guidman, wha's in sair need o' my help, and frae my mither, wha's deeing? Ye canna mean ye'll do that?"

Luckily the dim light did not permit her to see clearly the hideous grin which gradually overspread his features; but she saw enough to understand that she had failed to produce the effect she had intended. She had spoken in the hope of misleading him as to the extent of her suspicion of his guilt. But she soon learned that he was indifferent now as to how much she might know or suspect. Having got the notion that as she had overheard his conversation with the Laird, it was necessary to keep her beyond the reach of any chance of doing him injury, he meant to stick to it.

"Do you'll know," he said, in his slow way, rolling the words in his mouth as if he relished them, "I'll thocht you was a goot-looking lass, and I'll be goodmans and mithers and fathers and all to you. Yes—Pe-tam."

Bravely as she strove to curb all display of her loathing, she could not avoid shrinking back with a shudder.

"Are you cold?" he went on, to her infinite relief, making no attempt to touch her.

"Yes, it's a cold night; took a dram and that'll warm you."

He produced the bottle, which, after he had served the men and himself, he had placed in his pocket. She had recovered her self-possession, and she promptly held out her hand, took the bottle, and raised it to her lips. She gave it back to him as if she had taken a hearty waught, although she had not tasted the liquor.

"You'll know what's goot," he said, with satisfaction, "and here's your very goot health."

As she had calculated, he drunk copiously, and continued to drink at intervals as he spoke.

" Oich, but you'll hae the braw times, and the braw things to wear. Here's a braw schooner that'll run more fast than anything that's on the sea ; and she's all my own, and you'll be the mistress o' her, as I'm the master —your very goot health. I hae siller, too, and we'll go to the West Indies and the Africas, and you'll saw all the wonders o' the world, and we'll make a big lot o' siller out o' the niggers. Oich, it's a fine trade, and you'll hae the fine silks and all the braw things of all the world to wear. Yes—Pe-tam. And here's your very goot health again."

He emptied the bottle, but there was not the least perceptible change in his manner. She was disappointed, but his next words consoled her.

"You'll took some more—it's a cold night?"

She assented eagerly.

"Then come doon stair where I'll hae the barrel."

"I want to bide here a wee while yet."

"But it's cold, and I'll hae left your plaid on the shore."

"I dinna heed the cauld—but ye wouldna surely leave the schooner wi' just ae man on deck?"

"I'll forgot that. Donald's tooking a sleep, and I was to keep watch till he'll come up again. Grainger, he was a lazy swine, and will do nothing at all but shust what he'll no can help."

"Hae ye ken'd him lang?"

"Shust got him this morning at Ayr, and I would no had him if there was time to get any one other man, and if I'll know that he was so thrawart—Pe-tam—and here's your very—Oich, I'll forgot to go for the ouskie."

He descended to his cabin.

Jeanie immediately ran aft, looked over the stern to see if the small boat was still floating there.

It was gone.

She strained her eyes through the dim light, but there was no speck on the water within the range of her vision. She ran to the sides. But to her dismay the conviction was forced upon her that the hope she had entertained was destroyed. The boat had probably been insecurely fastened, the rope had slipped, and it had gone adrift.

The utter despair of that moment, the sickening sinking of the heart, stunned her.

But it endured only for a moment. A species of frenzied desperation took possession of her, and she stepped up to Grainger.

The man was sulkily attending to his duty, without having once looked toward her.

"Hae ye a wife, Mister Grainger?" she said, in a quick agitated voice.

"Aye, hae ye onything to say about her?" —(surlily.)

"Hae ye ony bairns?"

"Aye, what about them?"

"Do you ever want to see them again?"

The man stared in her face, puzzled.

"Has onything gaen wrang wi' them since I left hame?" he asked presently.

"No that I ken, but if ye ever want to see them ony mair, dinna sail wi' this boat."

"What's that got to do wi't?"

"Pe-tam—where was you?" shouted the skipper.

"Listen to what he says to me, but dinna speak or move unless I cry to ye."

She left the man, whose ill-humour had been startled out of him by her singular conduct and words, puzzled and wondering. She ran forward and seated herself on a coil of rope close by the hindmast, which was near

enough to Grainger to permit him to hear all
the conversation which might pass.

"I'm sitting doon here," she called in
answer to Carrach's repeated question as he
rolled about the deck seeking her.

"Oich, you was there," he said unsuspect-
ingly, advancing to her. "I'll thocht you
was somewhere. Here's a coat that'll keep
you warm, and here's twa bottles to keep my
ownsel' warm."

She put on the heavy jacket he had
brought her, permitting him to help her; and
she did not shrink or move when he sat down
close beside her. A desperate resolution had
grown out of her despair.

CHAPTER II.

CHECK.

"Come under my plaidie and sit doon beside me,
    I'll hap ye frae every cauld blast that can blaw;
Come under my plaidie and sit doon beside me,
    There's room in't, dear lassie, believe me, for twa."

Hector Macneil.

Ivan Carrach had in his own dull way a certain admiration for female charms, although he had never been a slave to them. Often his calf's eyes had rolled down the street after some trim lass; but the idea of making up to one had never entered his head; or, if it had, he had been always too much attached to his bottle to leave it and carry his idea into effect.

But here was a fine lass whom chance had placed in his way and necessity compelled him to take possession of, by whose side he could enjoy his bottle, and to reach whom he had not to take one step out of his usual course. Under these auspicious circumstances, he was tempted to play the wooer for once in his life. Hence his readiness to humour her by allowing her to remain on deck, especially as he did not see any possibility of her eluding him.

Naturally those things which appeared most pleasing to his own sight were the things which he fancied would be most pleasing to her. Consequently his wooing took the form of repeated assurances of the "braw gowns and things" he would get her, and a frequent proffer of drams, with a continual drinking of her "very goot health."

Jeanie suffered him to go on without exhibiting any of the loathing he inspired. She answered him quietly whenever it became necessary to make an answer, and she observed eagerly the rapid consumption of the whisky; but she was chagrined to find herself quite unable to detect any change in him. He drank and drank, but there was no apparent effect produced on him.

She began to be alarmed lest Donald should come on deck before she had made any successful movement, and she glanced uneasily at intervals towards the forecastle. But everything remained dark and silent there. Except Carrach's voice she only heard the splashing of the waves against the vessel and the occasional flapping of the sails in the wind.

He suddenly dropped his fat dirty hand on hers. Instinctively she started and drew back.

"What's the matter?" he said; "what did you'll got a start for?"

"Naething—I was just thinking about my folk at hame."

"Then think no more about them if that will make you start so. If you want onything to thocht about, thocht about me."

"I'm doing that."

"What more do ye want then? Shust look this way. I'm going to make a spoke, and you was the first lass I'll ever make a spoke to. Yes—Pe-tam."

" When is your other man to be up?"

" Oich, onytime; but it's no about him I'll want to spoke, it was about you, and no other body. You was the brawest lass I'll ever saw, and——"

" Did ye no say ye were gaun to the West Indies for the slave-trade?"

" Yes, but I was going to say——"

"When will ye be back in Scotland again?"

"Never, I'll thocht, unless I lose all my siller and my schooner, and am forced to come back to make the Laird get me another one."

" Would he do that? I heard him telling ye that he would hang ye if ye ever came his road again."

" Then we'll shust hang him too at the same time. But we'll no put him to all that trouble if we can help it."

" What has he done that you think you could hang him for?"

" That's no matter. I know what I know, and he's too big a coward to do what he said he would. But I was——"

"Has it onything to do wi' the murder o' Jeames Falcon?"

"Pe-tam," growled the Highlander, as if he had been stung, "Falcon was a brave boy, but he's dead, and I'll want to hear spoke of him no more."

"Ye didna like Falcon?"

"Well enough, well enough, but he was always pushing his nose into other folk's business, and that was a bother.   But, oich, he's dead, and here's his very goot health."

He took a deep draught from the second bottle, and smacked his lips with satisfaction when he had done.

Jeanie regarded him with a species of terror and marvel combined.   The only sensibility he had shown was at the first mention of Falcon's name; and then he had been moved rather as if an unpleasant personage had intruded on the conversation, than as one startled by a consciousness of guilt.   After that first uncomfortable movement, he had spoken in his ordinary slow way, with no other suspicious sign than might be seen in his unwillingness to continue the subject. She was at a loss to reconcile so much imperturbability with such a crime.

"The Laird didna like puir Falcon, I jalouse," she said presently, glancing over her shoulder, to make sure that Grainger was listening.

"The Laird was shust a tam coward, and was feared o' the lad."

"What for?"

The Highlander raised his dull eyes to her face, as if with some dim notion that she was cunningly trying to surprise his secrets.

"Shust for one thing and another," he answered, drinking again.

She understood his look, and did not press him farther on that point.

"I ay understood the Laird was a near man wi' his siller?"—(carelessly).

"So he was."

"But he wasna that wi' you frae what you hae said. He gied ye a hundred gowd pieces, did he no?"

"Yes, a hundred braw shining guineas"—

(with a guttural croak, intended for a chuckle of satisfaction)—"But that was shust because he was a tam coward, as I was told you, and he was feared to say no."

"And ye hae gotten a' the gowd in this ship"—(with affected surprise).

"Yes, all down stair in my locker. That was one reason what for I'll took you away with me, because I'll thocht you might do something to get them taken from me. But he'll be the brave lad and the clever lad that could get them now. Yes—Pe-tam"—(another croak and drinking).

The whisky was at last beginning to affect him, so far as to brighten his usually stolid manner with a degree of hilarity. But in other respects he was as deliberate and steady as ever.

Another glance round. Grainger had quitted the helm, and at first she could not make out where he had gone to; but presently lowering her eyes she perceived him stealthily approaching on his hands and knees behind Carrach. Her breath quickened. As she had calculated, the skipper's announcement of the destination and purpose of his voyage, and that he never intended to return to Scotland so long as the schooner served him, together with the revelation of the golden treasure which was lying down stairs, had roused some mutinous thoughts in the previously discontented mind of Grainger, which would be of service to her in assisting her to escape, if only Donald slept long enough.

"Ye hae got it a' in the locker o' your cabin," she went on; "and do ye think it's safe there?"

"Safe?—to be sure it was. There was nobody here to stole it; and if there was onybody, the locker's strong enough to hold against him; and if it was no, the door o' the cabin was stronger nor twa men. But, Petam, I'll want to spoke about yoursel'."

He attempted to put his arm round her waist. In spite of all her self-control she could not endure that. She started to her feet with a slight cry, springing back and facing him with alarm.

He sat still, staring in stupid surprise at her.

"What was it that you'll be feared aboot?" he said.

"Naething" (trembling and looking about as if seeking some weapon with which to defend herself. She started, and her eyes became fixed on one object at which she gazed straight over Carrach's head).

"Then come and sit doon again if you was feared aboot nothing. She'll no hurt."

"I canna come," she answered hesitatingly, and still gazing over him.

It was Grainger she was gazing at, and her mind was distracted between the terror of what was to happen, and the doubt whether she should interfere and lose the chance of escape which was opening to her, or leave the besotted skipper to his fate.

Grainger had risen to his feet, a belaying pin in his hand raised as if about to strike on Carrach's head.

A word from her might save him yet: her silence might be his death-warrant. The man paused, either to take surer aim or to make certain that she was not to interfere.

Her eyes were fixed upon him in the fascination of terrified suspense. She could not move or speak; but at a quick upward motion of his arm the horror of what was about to happen—of the thought that she was about to become accessory to a crime as black as that from which she was seeking to clear her husband—overcame all selfish care for her own safety, and she was on the point of shrieking out a warning to Carrach, who was still staring at her in perfect ignorance of the peril so near him, when she was unexpectedly spared the necessity of betraying the man on whose help she counted for release.

Grainger, at the very moment when he seemed gathering his strength for the blow, suddenly wheeled about, flung the belaying pin from him, and walked back with a surly swagger to the helm.

A load seemed to be lifted from her breast, and then she became perplexed, but not afraid now of the Highlander's love-making, for she was assured that very little provocation was needed to transform the steersman into an open mutineer.

At the noise caused by the rolling of the belaying-pin along the deck, Carrach turned himself round in the direction.

"What was you doing, Grainger?" he called.

No answer.

"Did you'll no hear what I was spoking?" cried the skipper, incensed.

"Aye, I hear; what would I be doing but minding the helm?" growled the man.

"You'll make the civil spoke afore very long while—Pe-tam."

He turned round again to Jeanie and once more invited her to resume her seat, but with a degree of gruff authority this time.

"Did ye no hear onything?" she said, pretending to listen.

"No—where?"

"I thought I heard the door o' your cabin shutting—is there a key in the lock?"

"Yes. What about that?"

"Gang doon and see; there's somebody below, I'm sure."

"There couldna be nobody there but Donald, and I didna see him go doon. But I'll look and fill the bottle again too."

He rose slowly, but quite as steady as usual, and moved toward the cabin. The instant his foot was on the first stair she darted over to Grainger.

"Ye heard what he said?" she whispered excitedly; "oh, will ye no help me for the sake o' the wife and bairns ye hae at hame?"

"Help ye to what?" (surly as ever).

"To win on shore."

"What for?"

"Did ye no hear? That man has done a murder, and I want to win hame to save him wha is falsely charged wi' the death o' James Falcon. Ye'll help me. For God's sake say ye will?"

"James Falcon murdered—I canna believe that."

She shrunk back a step. He seemed to
be ruthlessly crushing the hopes his conduct
had inspired in her.

"Did ye ken him?" she asked piteously.

There was a pause. Then growlingly—

"Aye, we sailed in the same ship thegither."

"And was he a friend o' yours?"

Another pause.

"Aye, a sort o' a friend."

"Then your friend lies cauld and dead, and
in his name I cry on ye to help me. He had
ay a true kind heart, and if he was your
friend ye maun hae ken'd that. He wouldna
hae said no to ane that was in sair distress
and needing help that he could gie, and
surely ye winna say no when I speak to ye
in his name."

"It's no sae lang since I saw him safe
enuch."

There was no tone of yielding in his gruff
voice.

"But I tell ye since then he's been stricken
doon—him that was ay brave and ready to

help others, was stricken doon in the dark,
and yon man's hand struck the blow. Oh,
will ye no believe me when I tell ye that
my ain man is lying in the jail enow charged
wi' the crime?"

"I dinna see what I can do for ye."

"I'll show ye what to do for me in a minute, and there's a' that gowd doon the stair."

"Aye, there's the gowd!"

"I'll no say a word about it, and he daurna;
sae that ye can hae it a' for yoursel'."

"I'll do what I can for ye."

"God bless ye for that."

She touched his arm gratefully with her
hand. She fancied that he was trembling;
but there was no time to think of that.

She ran to the cabin stair. There was a
light at the foot proceeding from the skipper's
room. She heard him tumble against some
bottles, and she was about to descend the
stair when the door opened, and he came
out.

The opportunity she had speculated on
seemed lost, but with a quickness which at any

other time would have amazed herself, she found an expedient.

"Hae ye looked if the gowd's a' safe in the locker?" she called to him.

"Oich, no, there was no need," he answered, looking up with his hand on the key of the door, which was placed in the lock on the outside, ready for him to turn it.

"Look and make sure," she said.

Muttering to himself he turned back. Her purpose was to lock him in, and then get Grainger to steer for the nearest port. Donald could easily be secured whilst he slept.

She glided down the stair swiftly, noiselessly. She closed the door and attempted to turn the key; but it had become displaced, and in the second occupied in replacing it the door was roughly pulled open, and Carrach clutched her wrist.

"What was you doing?" he said, with that croak of satisfaction. "Was you wanting to lock me up? Shust come in and see how you'll like it yoursel'."

She was so much overcome by this unexpected check to her stratagem, that at first she could not utter a word or cry for help. But as he rudely dragged her into the cabin, she gave vent to a shrill scream.

"That was no goot," he said, pushing her back; "did you'll thocht I didna see you make a spoke to Grainger? Oich, you was mistook then. So shust sit doon and I'll go and rouse Donald and come back to you. Yes—Pe-tam."

And he went out croaking with delight and locking the door upon her.

With another wild cry for help, which she thought Grainger must hear and answer, she dashed herself against the door trying to force it open. But it was strong, as the skipper had informed her when she had hoped to secure him by its aid, and she could not even shake it. She beat her hands helplessly against it with as little effect as a child's hand might have produced on a rock.

She fancied she heard the sound of a scuffle above, and she became still, listening intently. But if there had been any struggle between the men it was very brief, for it was over before she had collected herself sufficiently to listen.

She heard nothing but the monotonous plash of the waves against the timber, and the occasional rush of the wind as it swept in gusts over the vessel.

CHAPTER III.

SUSPENSE.

"Now wae to thee, thou cruel lord,
    A bluidy man I trow thou be;
For mony a heart thou hast made sair,
    That ne'er did wrang to thine or thee."—*Burns.*

Half an hour of agonizing suspense, and still Grainger did not come to release her. But neither did Carrach return as he had promised to do, and that was much to be thankful for, if she had not been suffering too acutely to find consolation in anything save positive rescue from the terrors which oppressed her.

By the dim light of the lantern swinging from the ceiling she searched the cabin for some instrument which might have assisted her to force the door; but she found none. She returned at last to the door and crouched down beside it, stupified and wretched. She had been so often that night within arm's reach of success, and she had been so often repulsed, that courage and hope seemed exhausted utterly.

In a dull dreary way she sought the meaning of her desertion. If Grainger had mastered the skipper he would certainly have come straight to the cabin to make sure of the gold. How promptly he had agreed to assist her when she had told him that it would all be his! What a potent fiend was this gold which could move men to any hazard who would not raise a finger to help a weary heart! She hated it, and yet a little while ago she had been grateful to it, for it had served in securing the surly Grainger. The ill-gotten store had seemed likely to work its own retribution, and at the last moment it had failed. Might it not succeed yet?

The question roused her. She had been in that half-waking state when thought passes through the mind by a mysterious and involuntary agency as in dreams. But that short sharp question had wakened her as if a drum had beat in her ear. She could form no idea of how long she had been dozing; but the lantern was burning dimly and flickering as it swung as if the oil were nearly burned out.

The soft rocking of the vessel, the plash, plash of the waves, and the whistling wind through the rigging, brought to her mind with many sharp pangs the dread reality of all that had passed, the cruel fear of all that might be to come.

She was chilled and stiff, so that she calculated she must have been a long while in the cramped position in which she found herself. She gained her feet with difficulty, and listened for any sound of human voice or movement which might betoken who was master of the schooner.

She covered her face with her hands. There was no gleam of hope to support her. Carrach must have roused Donald and with his help pinioned Grainger. He had not returned to her as he had threatened because he desired to be well out at sea before he again assailed her with his brutish wooing—a phase of his character which she deemed

more horrible than his darkest wrath or hate
could be.

She started back from the door; there was
a footstep on the stair; he was coming at last;
she glanced wildly round the chamber; there
was nothing with which she might defend
herself, nothing with which she might barri-
cade the door.

She clenched her teeth with desperate
resolve.   The strength of frenzy thrilled
through her veins.   She felt as if she were
strong enough to kill him if he touched her,
and she would do it.

The key was inserted in the lock.

She drew back as if prepared to make a
furious spring upon him and to gain the deck.
There she would be able to find some weapon,
and although it would be one woman against
two men, it would be a woman who was ready
to die.   She had forgotten Robin—everything
in the madness which possessed her.

The door opened cautiously.

" Are ye there?"

It was Grainger's voice.

It was well the man spoke. It was well
the tone was sufficiently distinct to enable
her to recognize it, for in another instant she
would have rushed upon him. Her tense-
strung nerves seemed to snap, and she sunk
to the floor weak, sobbing, and hysterical,
overcome by the excess of her relief.

"Are ye there?" repeated the man, and then
observing her he advanced with singular rapidity and raised her.

"What's wrang? Are ye hurt? Did he
touch ye?"

He spoke with an anxiety and respect
which even at that moment surprised her.

"No, no; but I thought it was him coming,
and I was ready to strike him dead if I could
—and when I knew it was you I got faint
wi' joy. Oh, what way did ye no come
sooner, or let me ken that he hadna got the
better o' you?"

As soon as he discovered that she was un-
injured save by her own terrors he placed her
on a seat and drew back, hanging his head
and answering as surlily as ever.

"I thought you would be the better o' a rest, and it was cauld on deck, and ye could hae been nae use there."

"Did ye no think o' the fear I would be in?"

"I just thought ye would be better down here nor on deck, and that was a'."

"Where is he then—how did ye do wi' him?"

"Easy eneuch. When he came up the stair I was waiting aboon wi' a rope ready, and I swung it ower him, and had him fast afore he could do mair nor get out a curse."

"Where is he noo?"

"I just drappit him into the hold. I didna want to hurt him mair nor I could help or I would hae felled him yon time on deck—aye, and I'd hae dune't if he had lifted a finger against ye. Lucky for himsel' sae far he didna do that, and lucky for me too, because I wanted to leave him wi' hale banes for the hangman. Sae, yonder he is noo in the hold without a broken bane, cursin' and swearin' like mad, but no able to steer hand or foot."

"And where is Donald?"

" Barred up in the forecastle. He's been kicking and growling too for the last hour, but I didna heed either o' them."

" What way did ye no come doon to tell me a' that afore? I hae been maist dead wi' fright thinking they had got ye doon as ye hae them. Were ye no anxious about the gowd ?"

" Oh—aye—yes. I was anxious about that"—(turning from her slightly as if looking for it, or desirous of hiding from her something peculiar in his manner).

" In the locker he said. I suppose that's it wi' the padlock ?"

" Aye, weel"—(hesitatingly)—" we'll just leave it there for the proper authorities to get it."

" What, are ye no gaun to take it yoursel' ?"

" Ye'll need it maybe to help to prove whatever ye want to prove against the man; and I'm content wi' getting safe out o' this boat. Thanks to your warning."

She regarded him now with astonishment mingled with pleasure. She felt more at ease than she had done since she had been seized by Carrach on the Links. But his generosity puzzled as well as amazed her. She could not understand how such a surly fellow as this could resist the temptation of wealth which lay at his hand for the lifting, merely because he thought it would be of service to her. She knew that it would be of much service in the proof against the Laird and Carrach. She had been willing to sacrifice that in order to tempt this man, and now she felt keenly ashamed of the motives she had attributed to him. Gold did not seem to be so omnipotent over the human heart after all.

"But ye can take it safely," she said, faltering, for she was shy of urging it upon him now.

"No, I wouldna take it, though it was to be nae use to ye."

She held out her hands to him, and as he made no movement to take them she laid them gently on his arm. Again she fancied he trembled, and this time it seemed to be at her touch.

"I ken now," she said with something swelling in her throat, "that Jeamie Falcon was a friend o' yours. Nae honest man ever ken'd him but liked him, and it's for his sake ye are helping me. I canna thank ye as I ought to do; but maybe it will be some satisfaction to ye to ken that Jeamie was ance mair nor all the world to me; and that but for the foul treachery o' yon man Carrach I might hae been his happy wife the-day. Ah, ye'll never ken what cruel sorrow that man has made us sup—Lord grant that ye never may, for then ye would wish that ye had died lang syne as I hae done mony a time."

She wiped her eyes, in which the first tears she had shed since that sad night at Askaig were trembling.

The man made no answer; but his head sunk lower on his breast in a gloomy way, and he backed to the door as if he wished to avoid her sorrow.

That reminded her of the weakness she

was displaying to a stranger who could not possibly sympathize with it, and she hastily tried to conceal it, as if it had been a thing to be ashamed of.

"Whereabout are we now?" she asked, trying to speak steadily, and bringing her mind back to the necessities of the moment.

"Come up and see," responded Grainger shortly, and he ascended the stair rapidly.

She followed. There was a pale misty gray in the sky: and a chill wind blowing, which intimated that dawn was at hand. Right ahead she saw two lights.

"What lights are they?" she asked.

"Portlappoch lights, and we'll be safe at anchor in less nor an hour if this wind hauds fair."

"Portlappoch?" she cried joyfully; "how did ye ken I wanted to gae there?"

"I just made for the nearest port that the wind would serve for," answered the man, turning away from her abruptly.

CHAPTER IV.

ANOTHER SURPRISE.

" Life ay has been a weary roun'
    Where expectation's bluntit,
Where hope gets mony a crackit crown,
    An' patience sairly duntit."

The wind did hold fair; and whilst the gray mists were still hanging heavy over the village, the schooner anchored in the port. Grainger had hailed a fishing smack, and obtained the assistance of a couple of men to take in sail and let out the anchor.

Before the fishermen came on board he had been assisted in everything he had had to do by Jeanie, who had worked with the energy of a man and the skill of a sailor. But he had scarcely spoken a couple of words to her from the time he had given her the pleasant tidings that she was so near home until now, when he was about to step on shore.

" Ye'd better bide here," he said, "till I send somebody to take charge o' the skipper and his mate, and syne ye can make sure they're safe in the right hands.'

He did not give her time for any reply, or to make any question about himself. He left her with the same surly abruptness his conduct had shown to her throughout.

She had little time to speculate on his strange ways, for she was speedily joined by Geordie Armstrong, big with his important share in the current events, and accompanied by half a dozen stout fisher-lads. Apparently he had received full instructions, for, without more than saluting Jeanie, he proceeded to his task. They seized Donald first, and he continued to offer all the resistance in his power, even after he was bound so fast that any attempt to escape was useless. He protested against arrest, as he had committed no crime; but Armstrong paid no more heed to him than to advise him to keep quiet and a civil tongue—advice which was quite thrown away.

Carrach at first resisted with all the strength desperation afforded him; but as soon as he discovered where he was, and in whose hands, he became doggedly silent, and in his bearing exhibited his ordinary stolid composure.

Armstrong left a man in charge of the schooner, and marched his prisoners off.

Jeanie waited until the last, expecting Grainger to return. But he did not come, and so she told the man in charge to bid him follow her to Mr. Carnegie, the writer's, if he should come back, and proceeded thither herself.

Mr. Carnegie was in his little business room or office, at his desk, with two candles shedding a sickly light in the misty dawn, which was creeping in through the window, on the paper on which he was writing with nervous rapidity.

On the other side of the desk stood a sailor-like man, who was answering the various questions the lawyer put in a sharp low voice at every pause of his pen. The man turned his head and stared at Jeanie as she entered. As soon as he had completed a sentence, Mr. Carnegie looked up too.

"You're early afoot, Mrs. Gray, but I'm glad to see you. I suppose you have learned something?"

She reported the extraordinary result of her visit to Clashgirn. At the first mention of Carrach and the schooner the sailor stared and eyed her curiously, but he did not speak. The lawyer, with his pen in his mouth, his elbows resting on the desk, and his head on his hands, listened without once interrupting her.

"You have had a lucky escape," he said when she had finished, "and a most extraordinary adventure. But I'm no astonished. I think I never will be astonished at onything in the world after this business. I'm glad you're safe through, and I'm glad you have gotten Carrach fast. And now you hae gotten him, I suppose you mean to charge him wi' the murder of James Falcon?"

"What else would I do?"

"And where's your proof? for, let me tell you at once, that although there are many things suspicious in what you have told me, there is nothing that in the least connects him with the murder. Then, where's your proof?"

She looked dismayed, but presently answered with decision.

"That we'll get from the Laird."

"That you'll no get from the Laird or onybody else," rejoined the lawyer firmly, as if it were a satisfaction to his legal mind to be able flatly to contradict even his own client —"supposing the Laird was willing to help ye instead of opposing you, he could not give you the proof if what this man says be true."

She turned upon the man angrily.

"And what is it he says?"—(she could only think that he came to bear witness against Robin, and that his evidence had been strong enough to affect even her agent).

"He just says the most astounding thing that was ever spoken on earth," said Mr. Carnegie, laying down his pen and giving the desk a rap with his knuckles, to emphasize his words and express his indignation at the idea of an enigma being presented to him which he could not solve, " he says that James Falcon has cheated us a second time, and that he's no dead ava."

Jeanie looked in bewilderment from one man to the other.

"What do ye mean?" she queried at length.

" That's just what I would like to know," ejaculated Mr. Carnegie, fidgetting with the indignation of one who has been hoaxed; "did you ever see this man before?"

" I dinna mind."

"Aye, well, his name's Hutcheson; he was the mate of the *Colin*, and he comes to me this morning to say that he has been with Falcon in Ayr for the last two days; that he only parted with him yesterday afternoon to come here to me by Falcon's order, and that Falcon himsel', instead o' lying a corpse at Clashgirn, is in hot pursuit of Ivan Carrach."

" Wha is't, then, that's lying there?"

" I'm fairly at my wit's end to guess. Everybody said it was Falcon."

" Did you see the body?"

" No"—(shuddering).

" Could you bear to look at it?"

A pause. Then—

" If it shouldna be him, would my guid-man win clear?"

" I could not answer that, but certainly it would be much in his favour if it should prove to be some one whom he had no motive for harming."

" Then I'll look at it, and I'll force the Laird to explain a' that is sae dark."

" I wish ye may. I'll be ready to go with you directly; I have just to settle one or two things about Carrach first."

" You'll no let him free?"

" No; although we cannot charge him with the murder, we can keep him fast on another charge. Hutcheson declares that, believing Falcon to be dead, and believing that his un-supported testimony as to the manner in which the *Colin* had been destroyed would only bring himself into trouble when opposed to the oaths of the skipper and the rest of the crew, he took a ship at Liverpool instead of returning home. But having now found Falcon alive, and, acting under his direction, he has come to me to declare what he knows of the event. In support of what he says there is one strong proof; namely, that the written statement which was presented to me by Carrach and signed William Hutcheson was never emitted by this William Hutcheson, some time mate of the *Colin*, and is consequently a forgery. Aha, we'll bind him tight enough on that count."

"Where is Jeamie Falcon?" she queried, still doubting, "and why does he no come here?"

"He'll no come here, mistress," said Hutcheson, speaking for the first time since her entrance. "When I parted wi' him yesterday afternoon, he bade me go back to Ayr as soon as I had made my statement to Mr. Carnegie, and to stop at the inn till I saw him again or heard frae him. Mr. Carnegie was to come to Ayr if he wanted to see him, for he had promised never to set foot in this place again."

Jeanie's face flushed.

"Do ye no ken where he is now?"

"I couldna say"—(awkwardly)—"but I can seek him if ye like."

"Seek him then, and tell him that it was me that begged and prayed him, for the sake o' a' that's gane and past atween him and me, to come back and save my guidman, wha lies in jail on his account."

"I'll do your will."

"Bring him here to Mr. Carnegie's. If it be true that he's living, he'll come when ye say that it was me wha sent for him."

"Sign this, Hutcheson," said Mr. Carnegie, "and then seek Falcon, and bring him here as quick as you can. We must have him here. That's the first thing you have got to do; and the first thing we have got to do, Mrs. Gray, is to learn who it is that has been murdered, and how the mistake of his identity has been made. Where is the man Grainger? We must keep him here till the fiscal comes."

Jeanie could not tell where he was, and a

messenger was despatched in search of him. Hutcheson departed, promising to return as soon as he should meet Falcon, or learn his whereabouts.

She was too eager to take the next step in the strange journey she was making—a journey which was distracted by so many unexpected turns and mazes, and the end of which was yet so dark—to think of rest. The lawyer, however, was not a man to forget such a material element of life as breakfast; and so he presently folded up his papers, laid down his pen, and invited Mrs. Gray into the parlour, where his morning meal was waiting for him.

"I can neither eat nor rest," she said, "until something has been done to gie me assurance o' Robin's safety."

"Aye, but you'll try to do both. When there's serious work to be done, Mrs. Gray, ye should never set about it fasting. Hunger, though you may not feel it, or ken how it works on you, shortens the temper and the patience, and for that very reason weakens the judgment, and loses the thread o' the argument that might lead to the conclusion you want. You will have need of both cool reason and patience, so come awa' ben and lay the foundation o' them wi' a hearty breakfast."

He led her into the parlour, and if she did not make a satisfactory repast it was not her host's fault. When they had finished, he rose—

"Now," he said kindly, "you'll rest here till I come back. I'm going to see Carrach. I must be candid with you, and beg you not to expect too much from what we have learned. What this man Hutcheson says, although it makes the business of the *Colin* quite clear so far as the skipper is concerned, scarcely affects McWhapple, for we have nothing to show that he had entered into a conspiracy with his skipper, except the inference that he was likely to have done so, as he was the greater gainer of the two in the destruction of the brig. But that is mere inference."

"Carrach will confess."

"I hope he may. But then as regards your guidman, Hutcheson's news just raises more difficulties about it, and there were enough before, I'm sure. I confess honestly that I'm more puzzled how to proceed in this matter than I ever was in the whole course of my experience."

"But surely, sir, when they find that Falcon is living, they canna make out ony reason for my guidman wishing to harm ony other body?"

"Would you like to ken what the fiscal would say to that? He would just gie one o' his cheery smiles that seem to me ay to be deluding folk wi' the notion that he's only speaking in fun when he's in dead earnest, and he would tell you that there has been a man killed and not by an accident. Robin Gray was the only man known to be about the place at the time except Robert Keith. Against the latter there is nothing to raise suspicion; against the former everything testifies. Whether a motive for the crime is discovered or not, we must have some better proof than his own assertion that his was not the hand that throttled the man, and then heaved him over the precipice, before the evidence against him can be upset. That's what the fiscal would say."

Jeanie sighed.

"Very well, sir (quietly), we will hae to find the better proof that's needed."

The lawyer regarded her admiringly, and pityingly too.

"Nothing daunts you?"

"Nothing could daunt me but seeing him on the scaffold, kenning that he, innocent, was to die the death o' shame, and I, his wife, had failed to save him."

There was such a radiant light of love and faith over her simple upturned face that the old man felt his blood tingle with admiration.

"Ods, my life, I never thought there was so much endurance in a' the women in the world. It'll no be my fault if we fail. I'll be back as quick as I can; and I'll get the gig brought to the door, so that we can start the minute I'm ready. A' that has been said just brings us back to where we started: before we can move a step we must learn who is the dead man."

"Before ye gang, Mr. Carnegie, tell me ae thing: supposing that Mr. Hutcheson had someway made a mistake, and supposing that it *was* Jeamie Falcon that was killed, would no what ye hae learned about the *Colin* help to shift suspicion frae my guidman?"

"Of course it would."

An hour elapsed before he returned. He found her pacing the floor with flushed and excited face. She greeted him with a cry of joy.

"I ken it a', sir, I ken it a' now," she cried.

"How—what—?"

"The body that was found the folk a' said was Jeamie Falcon's," she went on rapidly, "they believed it was him, sae that there must have been something about it to make them so sure."

"Yes, what then?"

"Carrach went to Askaig by stealth to

kill Jeames Falcon, and in the dark mistook this man for him!"

She looked at him, her eyes bright with the enthusiasm of discovery and conviction. A pause. Then—

"That may be," he said thoughtfully; "but say nothing about it at present. The argument cuts two ways, and might be used against as well as for Cairnieford."

" Hae ye learned naething frae Carrach?"

" Naething; he's as dour and speechless as a Highland stirk; he comes of the breed."

" We'll find a way to gar him speak yet," she ejaculated determinedly, and accompanied her friend to the door where the gig was waiting.

As they were seating themselves, the lad who had gone to seek Grainger came back with the intelligence that the man could not be discovered anywhere in the town.

" Odd," muttered the lawyer, and drove away.

CHAPTER V.

FOUND.

> " Hear ye the heart-sick soun's that fa'
> Frae lips that bless nae mair;
> Like bieldless birdies when they ca'
> Frae wet wee wing the batted snaw,
> Her sang soughs o' despair."—*W. Thom.*

As they neared Clashgirn they became aware that some unusual occurrence was going forward. Groups of men, whose sombre garments and still more sombre countenances intimated that they had come to attend the funeral, were standing about discussing some topic of more than ordinary interest, and one associated with the house, as their frequent glances toward it showed. There was a goodly gathering already, and all had not arrived yet; for James Falcon had been much liked by the country-folk, who felt it to be a duty—whether invited or not—to pay him the last testimony of their good-will by following his body to the grave.

Many salutations were given to the lawyer as he drove by, but none offered to stay him or to explain the subject of their gossip. As they descended at the door, which was wide open, a man took the reins of the horse and said in a low tone—

"Ye'd better just gang ben, Mr. Carnegie; for I dinna think ye'll see onybody to ask ye in the noo."

They entered and encountered Mrs. Begg, who was descending the stair crying and wiping the tears from her eyes with her apron as fast as they rose.

"Eh, Mistress Gray!" she exclaimed the instant she caught sight of her, "what gar'd ye gie me sic a fright? What did ye gang awa' for without telling me?"

"I'll tell ye a' about that anither time—hae they nailed doon the—coffin yet? I want to see him that's in't."

"For guidness sake dinna gang up the stair enow—ye'll never get the better o't. My head's in a reel, and Girzie Todd's came and turned a' thing and a' body tapsalteerie.

I dinna ken what's gaun to happen neist, but
surely the world's coming to an end. I wish
we may a' be forgien, but it's an awful thing
to think o', and—"

"Come up," interrupted Mr. Carnegie
briskly.

Without giving Mrs. Begg time to explain
her incoherent ejaculations, he hastened up
the stair and Jeanie followed him.

From the chamber at the head of the staircase issued low moans as of one in agony.
He pushed open the door, and they entered.
But the spectacle before them brought them
to an abrupt stand-still when they had barely
crossed the threshold. At the farthest corner
stood the Laird behind a chair, which served
as a support for him in the absence of his
staff. His pale foxy eyes were blinking excitedly at the intruder; and with his hands
he gesticulated wildly to him (from his position he only saw Mr. Carnegie at first) as if
warning him to retire. But as soon as he
caught sight of Jeanie close behind the lawyer, his hands dropped heavily on the chair,

and he blinked at her with a blank scared visage.

When he had been warning Carnegie he seemed afraid or unwilling to speak lest he should disturb the second person in the chamber; but when Jeanie showed herself he seemed unable to speak.

A little nearer the door the coffin had been placed on four chairs—it was too long to fit into the box-bed. The lid had not yet been nailed on; the covering had been torn down, and across the ghastly remains, the arms clutching the sides of the shell with a fierce grip, lay a woman moaning piteously. Her hair dishevelled, her clothes disarranged, the eloquent negligence of her position and ignorance of all that was passing around her, indicated what paroxysms of anguish she had passed through.

It was Girzie Todd, and, like all strong natures, when once abandoned to grief, it became terrible to hear her alternate childish complainings and bursts of fury.

"Aye, aye, what was an auld fisherwife's

brat to them?" she was sobbing in low hoarse
tones; "what did they ken or care that ye
was day and sun and life to her? My ae
lamb, my bairn, my bairn. . . . Can ye
hear me noo?   Do ye ken that I'm crying to
ye, and will ye no say a word to me? . . .
Dawnie will miss ye sair at supper-time—and
oh, what a toom world ye hae left to me.
. . . And the folk dinna care; they'll glower
at me maybe, but syne they'll jist gang on
wi' their wark as though there was naething
wrang. Wattie, my bairn, in dule and
shame ye cam'; in dule and shame ye hae
been taen awa, and naebody minds that ye're
dead but your lone mither."

Her sobs choked all further utterance for
a few minutes. Abruptly she started up, her
eyes kindling to fury as she gazed wildly on
the mangled form.

"Dead? Oh, and sic a death! My bonnie
harmless bairn, sae hashed that your ain
mither daur scarcely look on ye, that your
ain mither can barely tell it's you"—(with
rising passion). "But, as there's a God

aboon, the hand that struck ye doon shall wither on the gallows - tree — I'll see the corbies pick his banes till he's mair fricht-some to look on than ye are lying there."

"For Heaven's sake, woman, be quiet," ventured the trembling Laird, whose awe of the woman's despair was overcome by the fear that she might say something he would not wish the listeners to hear.

"Quiet! and that lying forenenst me!" (her hand swept over the coffin, whilst a look of angry contempt was cast on the man). "Ye can cry quiet, ye puir mouse-hearted creature, though it's your ain wean that's been foully done to death! I'll no be quiet until the hand that has wrought this ill-work is blighted, and his name is trodden under foot."

And as she stamped her foot on the floor, it touched a heap of old tattered clothes which was lying near. The touch brought her eyes to them, and her fury changed to piteous moans, as she sunk down beside the heap, fondling the garments, and murmuring over them as if they had been living things. She had not yet observed the presence of Mr. Carnegie and Jeanie.

The former advanced to her now, and touched her on the shoulder.

"Girzie," he said kindly, "I have heard what you were saying—"

"But the woman's demented wi' her sorrow," shrieked the Laird, "ye canna believe a word she says."

Girzie turned on him fiercely.

"Why can he no believe what I say? Are ye feared that I mean to seek onything frae you? or are ye feared yet that folk should ken that the puir daft Wattie was your bairn? I would skirl it frae ae end o' the toon to the other if I wasna mair shamed for his father nor I ever was for him."

"She's raving——"

"Raving?—ye say that" (with a bitter laugh), "I was raving ance and daft tae; that was when I believed ye was an honest man. But that's twenty years syne, and in a' that weary while I hae never sought bite

or sup frae ye for me or my bairn, nor hae I
ever tauld the folk what a fause leeing hypo-
crite I ken'd ye to be. It's no worth my fash
to do't noo. I scorned the siller that ye
would hae gien me to gang awa' frae the place
lang syne, and I would do't again. Aye, I
would stap thir hands atween twa mill-stanes
afore I would let them touch a bodle's worth
o' your gear."

"Never heed the Laird or the bygane just
now, Girzie," interrupted Mr. Carnegie. "Let
them rest for a minute, and see if you can be
calm enough to answer me a few questions."

"Oh, aye, I'm calm enuch, but is't no a
queer thing, Mister Carnegie, that ony woman
in her senses could ever hae thocht twice
about sic a shiverin' creatur' as yon, that
winna even steer a foot when he kens his ain
flesh and blood has been murdered. But it's
true though" (with a harsh bitter laugh).
"I ance believed in him, and lippened to him,
and got the reward I micht hae expected.
When he got to be Laird, he couldna marry
a puir servin' lass, the dochter o' Hieland

fishers, though she was the mither o' his bairn. But he would hae gien me siller to gang awa', sae that the session micht never get word o't, and he micht marry some braw leddy, aiblins. But I bode here and I held my tongue just for the pleasure o' torturin' his coward soul wi' the sicht o' me. The langer I held my tongue the mair feared was he, and he daurna marry as he wanted, just because I was watchin' him. Oh, it was some satisfaction for the wrang he had done me to ken that he was under my thoomb, and that ony day I could shaw the folk what a black knave he was, although I would hae been sair shamed to own that sic a creatur' was the father o' my puir Wattie that's lying cauld and mangled there. O Lord, *he* has been sair punished for the sin that wasna his, and through him, me, and aiblins through us baith, the man wha wranged us."

The recollection of the past shame and sorrow, all mention of which she had so long suppressed, seemed now in its utterance to relieve the anguish of the present; and her tone became harsher and clearer as she proceeded, in spite of every effort of the lawyer to interrupt her. The singular disclosure, which, although it surprised him, and at any other time would have excited his curiosity in reference to one who had been so long regarded as a paragon of morality, did not seem to bear upon the purpose he had in view at this moment, and he was anxious to dispose of it as quickly as possible.

"Well, well, but Girzie," he said testily, "if you want to punish the criminal, as you say, will you listen to me?"

"Oh, aye, I hear."

She spoke with indifference now—for her mood changed from passion to despair every instant—and she flung herself across the coffin again, hiding her face.

The Laird, as if relieved by her prostration, nervously sat down on the chair he had been keeping before him as if for a barrier in the event of the woman in her frenzy attacking him, and took several pinches of snuff in rapid succession, but quietly, as if he were afraid of making the least noise to remind Girzie of his existence. He was calling all his cunning to his aid to find some expedient whereby he might shield himself from the contumely her revelation would bring upon him — for, as the woman understood, his terror of it grew and multiplied with the years it lay hidden in proportion to his own advance in respectability. He was busy, too, noting the conversation which followed. Every word had its importance to him.

"I came here expressly," Mr. Carnegie resumed, "to learn whether or no it was true that there had been a mistake in the identity of this unlucky man. Now tell me, how do you know that this is your son Wattie and not James Falcon?"

"Hoo do I ken? Ah, man, I would hae ken'd my puir laddie though they had hackit him in pieces."

"Aye, aye, but how would you have known him—was there any mark on his person, any sign by which you could have distinguished him without the help of his features?"

"He was my bairn, I tell ye; isna that eneuch?"—(doggedly).

"For you, Girzie, no doubt, more than enough, but not enough for the law in the face of the evidence of several persons that it was James Falcon."

"It was the claes they looked at, no the man. Do ye think they would look at him as I hae done?"

"Then you admit that the clothes were Falcon's?"

"Aye, nae doubt o't."

"Then how could he come to be dressed in another man's clothes?"—(This with a degree of the satisfaction a cross-examiner experiences when he thinks he has pinned a witness.)

"I dinna ken and dinna care. A' that I ken is that this morning I found up by at Askaig thae claes that are lying at my foot, and they were Wattie's, sae that he couldna hae had on his ain, and maun hae had on some ither body's."

"Come, Girzie, try to be calm for his sake,

and tell me exactly how you came to make this discovery. You went away two or three days ago to seek Wattie; that was before the body was found. Now, begin there and tell me all about it."

"I gaed awa' on Wednesday night to Ayr, kenning that Falcon would gang there to sail for the south, and believing that Wattie was alang wi' him. On Thursday morning I found out that a boat had sailed for England on the Tuesday, and there wasna another to sail for an English port till the-day."

"Now we're getting at it properly. You may be sure, Girzie, I would not harass you this way if it could be helped; but it is positively necessary that we should be certain this time as to the identity of the man."

"I ken'd that he couldna hae sailed on the Tuesday, and that unless he gaed by the coach or went on to Stranraer, he couldna be out o' the toon. I gaed to the coach-office, and he hadna travelled that way, for they hae the names o' a' the folk in a book. I wandered aboot the town seeking him and

my laddie, but I couldna hear onything about
ane or ither till yester-e'en."

"Well, what did you learn then?"

"I fell in wi' a chield ca'ed Hutcheson,
wha was ance mate o' the *Colin* that was
burnt, and he tauld me that he had just
parted wi' Jeamie Falcon, and that my laddie
wasna wi' him, and hadna been wi' him.
Hutcheson ken'd that, for him and Falcon
had been biding thegither frae the day afore.
I waited nae langer nor to ken that Hutcheson was coming to our toon the day, and
that Falcon was to meet him again at Ayr.
Syne I started for hame, thinking I might
find Wattie there."

"You started last night?"

"Aye; but I had travelled ower far as it
was, and was clean forfauchen, sae that I lay
down by a dyke-side, and couldna move till
a cottar found me and took me into her
house, whar I bode a' night. This morning
I cam' in by Askaig, thinking I might find
some news o' him there. Rab Keith told me
about the murder o' Jeamie Falcon, as was

thocht. But my heart misgied me, for I
ken'd that Falcon was living. I gaed to look
at the place where the man had been thrown
ower the Bite, and coming back to the road
we passed the shed that was blawn down.
Rab had been clearing awa' the timber, and
in ae place he showed me he had just found
this morning a bundle o' auld claes. They
were lying there yet, and when I saw them I
ken'd they were Wattie's, and I jaloused mair
and mair that it was him had been got in
the burn."

"What did you do?"

"I speired whar the body was, and came
here to find that what I feared was ower true,
that it was my laddie, wha never harmed
living creature, had been struck doon. There
was his hand, I couldna mistake that wi' the
wart on the left thoomb, and there is a pickle
o' his bonnie hair. If the folk that said it
was Falcon hadna been misled wi' the claes
they would hae minded that Falcon's hair
was far darker nor that."

"You have just given us the very proof

that was wanted. Now, Mrs. Gray, perhaps you can recollect what clothes Wattie had on when you last saw him at Askaig?"

Jeanie had been standing all this time on the threshold, listening and observing the Laird, but not advancing because of the sickening thought of what lay in the coffin, the top of which she could just see. Behind her was Mrs. Begg, who had been ordered out of the room by the Laird when he had dreaded the coming disclosure. He had done so with sufficient spleen to cause her to go downstairs crying; but she had immediately followed the visitors up again, and her horror and indignation at the revelation of her master's baseness (mingled with thankfulness that she had escaped the union she had some time coveted) were with difficulty restrained. Only the fear of being driven downstairs a second time and missing what was to follow enabled her to control her tongue.

Jeanie hesitatingly advanced two steps into the room, with eyes averted from the coffin.

Girzie, from whom she had hitherto been concealed by the open door, observing her now, started up, with a return of her fierce bitter manner.

"Oh, ye're there, Mistress Gray," she cried. "Come awa' ben, woman, come awa' ben and see the fine handiwark o' your guidman. Eh, but it'll be a braw sicht to see sic a sturdy chield swinging in the air, and ye'll be at liberty to marry Jeamie Falcon yet for nae mair cost nor the life o' daft Wattie Todd."

The cruelty of this speech rendered Jeanie dumb for the moment. But then recovering herself, she turned upon the distracted mother with indignation that overwhelmed all commiseration.

"Wha says that Robin Gray is to blame for this? and what would he meddle wi' your son for—him that was ay a guid frien' to baith o' ye?"

"Oh I ken a' about it. He didna think it was my Wattie he was dinging ower the crag; but whether he thocht it or no he'll hing for't. I ken noo what he was in sic a

sair way aboot, and what he was in sic haste
to win awa' for; but we'll send him on a
langer journey nor he expeckit."

"Toot, toot, Girzie," interrupted the lawyer sharply, "you must not take the whole
business of judge and jury into your own
hands this way, when the affair is puzzling
cooler heads than yours. Just never heed
her, Mistress Gray, ye see she's distracted with
what has happened. Tell us about the
clothes."

"I couldna say what clothes he had on. I
was ower muckle fashed at the time to notice
onything o' that kind. But let me tell ye,
Girzie, that my man had nae mair ado wi'
this wicked wark nor ye had yoursel'."

Girzie laughed a harsh mocking laugh.

"Wha do ye think had to do wi't
syne?"

"Speir at the Laird there, whase guilty
conscience keeps him trembling like a strae
in the wind. He kens wha did it and how
it was done."

"Him!" shrieked Girzie.

"Aye, him. Do ye no see the guilt o't in his face?"

And true enough there was a ghastly terror expressed on his sallow visage as he rose to his feet, his lips moving as if he were about to offer some defence, but no sound coming from them.

Girzie strode up to him, griped his arm savagely, and glared at him.

"Is this your wark?" she said hoarsely, dragging him close to the coffin.

It was a critical moment for him: Jeanie and the lawyer were watching him; and Girzie was noting every quiver of his features. But as if the enormity of the charge brought against him had restored all his cunning wits to their proper balance, he suddenly became the most collected person in the room.

"Mr. Carnegie," he said quietly, "would ye oblige me by crying up some o' my loons till we get this woman taken care of. She's no fit to be at liberty, that's clear; and as for Mrs. Gray, she's either losing her senses too,

or she's been very much misled by her suspicions."

"Is this your wark?" repeated Girzie
darkly. "Has the father's hand taen the
bairn's life, and is the sin committed sae lang
syne to be brought hame to us at last in this
awfu' way?"

"I'm sorry for ye, Girzie, and I can excuse
ye a heap on account o' the wrang I did ye;
but I would hae made amends for it if you
would hae allowed me. But we'll let that
pass, and I'll answer your question just because I'm sorry for ye, and would satisfy you
if I could. I had nae hand in this dreadful
deed."

He spoke with so much meekness, and with
such an air of sorrow for the bereaved mother
whilst admitting the truth of her previous
statement, that it seemed impossible to doubt
him. Even Jeanie was staggered.

Girzie with some dim recollection of the
old superstitious test of a suspected murderer's
innocence by causing him to touch the body
of the victim, when, if guilty, the blood

flowed afresh, but if innocent there was no change—released his arm, and said sternly—

"Place your hand on his breast, and swear before Heaven that ye had nocht ado wi' this by thocht, or word, or deed."

A scarcely perceptible shudder passed over him, but he instantly complied.

"To please ye, Girzie, I'll do that, though it's a ridiculous thing even to want me to do't. There, my hand is on his breast, puir lad, and I had nothing to do with his misfortune. I declare it solemnly, as I hope for mercy."

There was a brief silence, through which only the heavy breathing of Girzie was heard. Her eyes were fixed upon him with a wild stare, marking how much she would have liked to believe, and yet how much she doubted even this solemn declaration.

"Aye, ye can say that about Wattie Todd," broke in Jeanie, passionately; "but ye couldna and ye daurna hae said it if it had been Jeamie Falcon that was lying there."

"And why no, Mistress Gray? Why would I no hae daured to deny this ridiculous charge if it had been Falcon that lay there? Falcon, the puir friendless bairn that I brought up at my ain expense, that I looked on wi' as muckle regard as though he had been my ain, and wha I was meaning to make heir o' Clashgirn and a' I possess, as your friend, Mr. Carnegie, can testify."

"That's true," said the lawyer, as if remembering an important fact he had quite forgotten. "On Thursday, before anything was suspected of this business, the Laird gave me instructions to draw up his will in favour of James Falcon."

"And I would think," added the Laird, with a complacent dab of the head, "that fact will be accepted as some proof that I could hae had no thought of harming the lad."

Again Jeanie was staggered. She had expected to surprise him into confession, or at least some explanation which would betray his knowledge of the crime; and instead of that she seemed to be only bringing to light proofs to confound her own convictions. She could see that both Girzie and Mr. Carnegie were impressed by the Laird's last words. But, with a sort of instinctive logic, her mind presently grasped the one assailable point of this evidence.

"No," she cried, her face flushing with fancied triumph, "the fact will be accepted as proof that ye ken'd what had happened before onybody else, and that ye just gied orders for your will to turn a' suspicion awa' frae ye——"

"Mistress Gray——"

But she would not be interrupted——

"Aye, ye may weel haud up your hands and look horrified, for ye ken I'm speaking the truth. What would ye harm the lad for? ye say wi' your fause tongue. Because he ken'd how the *Colin* was burnt, and baith you and Carrach were feared for your lives. If that wasna sae—if the murder o' that puir lad that was mista'en for another doesna lie atween you and Carrach—what was the meaning o' your stealing awa' like a thief frae your ain house last night to meet him on the Links? What was the meaning o' your pay-

ing him a hunder pieces o' gowd, and threat-
ening that if he ever came back ye would
deliver him ower to the hangman? What
was yon paper ye gar'd him put his mark till
and me sign my name on? and what did ye
allow him to carry me awa' for when ye found
out that I had been watching ye? What
for, but that the guilt on your conscience
made ye ready for ony deed that might
hide it."

Girzie had been standing with darkly
troubled visage, glowering alternately at the
Laird and Jeanie. At the mention of Carrach's name she had started, shuddering, and
a light had seemed to flash over her face.

"Ivan Carrach!" she now ejaculated hoarsely,
" he is my brother—whar is he?"

Jeanie was too much excited to notice the
new source of surprise and complication in
Girzie's announcement of her relationship to
the Highlander. She answered triumphantly,
for she fancied the answer would shake the
Laird's last support, and her eyes were fixed
on him steadily the while—

" He's a prisoner, fast bound, in the care o'
Geordie Armstrong."

Girzie stood an instant gazing blankly at
the speaker; then, clenching her teeth, she
strode out of the room, not looking to right
or left, not even giving a parting glance at
the coffin.

CHAPTER VI.

BAFFLED.

"Like a saint sincere and true
He discovered all he knew,
And for more there was no occasion."
                              Jacobite Ballad.

Girzie's interruption had given the Laird
a breathing space. When first made aware
of Carrach's arrest, his weak eyes had blinked
a little more than usual. But that was all; for
he had been expecting to learn that some accident had befallen the skipper from the
moment he had seen Jeanie at the door.
Consequently, he was in a manner prepared
for the announcement. Besides, although an
utter coward when any physical danger was
close upon him, so long as there was time for
cunning to serve him, his foxy craft had re-
sources enough for the occasion.

He utterly astonished Jeanie, and perplexed the lawyer, by producing his snuff-box, taking a refreshing pinch, and sighing with all the resignation of a martyr who feels that his long-suffering spirit has been driven to extremity, and that it must now assert itself in the cause of truth.

"Od, it's extraordinar'!" he exclaimed meekly, gently raising his hands and dabbing his head, "that the most innocent and kindly-meant actions o' ane's life may be turned against him like whips to scourge him. Mistress Gray, I wonder at ye, and I'm sorry for ye too. Will ye please to step down the stair to my room, and I'll gie ye a' the explanations that are in my power? I dinna like to stand here disgracing the presence o' the dead wi' our unseemly squabbles. Will ye kindly respect my scruples on this point and oblige me?"

As is usual when one is excessively angry, humble politeness on the part of the person who has roused our anger acts on the system much like a dip in cold water. Although his submission only intensified her loathing for the creature, she was unable to offer any opposition to his moderate and polite request. She simply followed Mr. Carnegie, who immediately complied with the Laird's wish.

As soon as they had entered the chamber below, the Laird closed the door, placed a chair for Jeanie, and observing that she looked fatigued, asked in his mildest tone if she would allow him to offer her some slight refreshment. She was for the moment dazed by his marvellous placidity, and the respect with which he treated her, notwithstanding the grave imputations she had brought against him, and she could not have answered him even had she been disposed to do so. Neither would she sit down.

He did not press her; but after giving Mr. Carnegie a chair, he produced bottle and glasses from his cupboard, and asked him to partake. The lawyer, from being puzzled, begun to feel a little awkward under the circumstances, and accepted the hospitality. Never in all his experience had he seen or

heard of a guilty person conducting himself
with such equanimity and friendliness toward
his accusers.

"Now, Mrs. Gray," said the Laird meekly,
with another pinch and another dab, and
seating himself, so that he should face both
his hearers, " it shall no be my fault if I dinna
gie ye satisfaction in respect o' everything ye
suspect. Your suspicions canna harm me.
I hope I hae spiritual strength enough to bear
far mair if necessary for the sins o' the flesh
I hae committed.   But I'm wae to think o'
what a dreadful state o' mind ye must be in
before ye could hae gien sic suspicions breath.
I'm sure it would be the height o' pleasure
to me if I could relieve ye in ony way.
Aiblins it will help ye a wee thing if I clear
up everything sae far as I can in a prompt
and plain manner."

He paused, as if expecting her to commend
his frankness; but she did not move or speak.
She only continued to look straight in his
face, wonderingly.

"That's all we require, sir," said Mr. Car-

negie, feeling that some reply was demanded;
" and all that is necessary."

The Laird took a complacent pinch, and
proceeded.

" Weel, I'll say naething about the very
great boldness o' stepping into a man's house
—especially when that man was ay ken'd as
ane wha feared the Lord and walked upright
—and making sic wild charges against him,
wi' very little proof to back them, as it seems
to me. I'll say naething about that, although
the very serious nature o' the charges will
compel me to insist on the fullest investigation o' my conduct, if ye persist in them after
my explanation. Should that investigation
be onyway to the detriment o' your guidman's cause—as I doubt it will be—I take
Mr. Carnegie to witness that a' the blame is
your ain."

He paused again, and still she did not
speak.

" Mrs. Gray has no doubt said more than
she meant," explained the lawyer, fidgetting,
and beginning to think that he had been

somewhat hasty in falling in with her suspicions, to the grave injury of his professional
reputation and business; "she was excited,
sir, as you could not help observing, by the
vexatious words of Girzie Todd."

"Oh, I make a' needful excuses, dinna fear
that, Mr. Carnegie; and I declare to ye there's
nae anger in my heart against Mistress Gray,
for I ken the troubled state o' her mind, and
as I hae told ye I'm sorry for her."

"I dinna need your pity," she said, in a
low unsteady voice; "I want to hear your
explanation."

"Ye'll no hae to wait lang for that, then,
Mistress Gray. We'll begin at the beginning,
and regarding what ye hae said about the
Colin, I cannot understand you. But on that
score ye couldna hae a better adviser than
Mr. Carnegie, for the brig was assured through
him, and it's both his business and his interest
to make sure that there was naething wrang
in the way the vessel was lost. I will insist
upon him going over the evidence as to her
loss again, and although I was only a part

holder in her, I pledge mysel' to make guid
every penny o' the insurance money, wi' due
interest, if there has been the least unfair
dealing."

"Ye may be ca'ed on to answer for't wi'
something mair nor your siller," she said, beginning to beat the floor with her foot.

"We'll soon ken that, for I'll place the
matter in the hands o' the fiscal mysel' this
very day. Now, respecting last night: it's
quite true I quitted the house at a late hour,
but no to my knowledge wi' ony difference
in my manner frae my usual way of going
out when necessary, and coming back when
I like. No being a married man, there's
naebody to question my incoming or outgoing."

"Ye looked unco like as if ye were feared
o' onybody kenning o' your outgoing."

The Laird only smiled benignantly, and
blinked upon her, tapping his snuff-box the
while.

"Ye were watching me, and ye wouldna
hae been watching me if ye had no suspected

that I had done something wrang. Your ain suspicion would gie my manner a' the peculiarity ye attach to it. Very weel, I'll no stop to argue wi' ye; I'll just tell ye what I was doing and why I was doing it, and I may just say at the same time that I hae proof enough to satisfy ony unprejudiced person o' the truth o' what I say."

" I judge ye by what I saw and heard."

" And judge me wrang, as ye'll admit some day. I gaed to the Links and met Carrach, as ye hae said—and if ye please, ye'll mind how easy it would be for me to deny a' this, seeing that it's only your word against mine, and yours is the word o' an interested person. But I frankly own to everything ye hae said, barring the conclusions ye hae drawn, of course."

"Oh, aye, that *looks* honest," she said bitterly.

"Od, it's extraordinar'," exclaimed the Laird, taking another pinch, and looking appealingly to the lawyer, "how suspicion will distort the plainest facts. However, I feel it's my duty to try and satisfy ye, although the sinful pride o' man tempts me to bid ye gae your way, and no to say another word to ye. But I'll no do that. I hae admitted that I met Carrach on the Links—"

"And gied him a hunder gowd pieces?"

"Surely, seeing that I drew them frae the bank for him yesterday. Now, I'll tell ye why. Ye mind, Mr. Carnegie, speirin' yesterday, when ye met me at the door o' the bank, where Carrach was, and when I expected to see him?"

"Perfectly, and you said you thought he was at Ayr, and that you expected him at Portlappoch to-day, although you could not be sure of it."

"Just that. Weel, when I got hame here yesterday afternoon there was a message waiting me frae Carrach, to say that he couldna clear out o' Ayr till the evening, that about twal o'clock he would be opposite the Links, and if I would bring the siller there, and signal to him, he would come ashore and take it frae me and gie me a receipt, as he wanted to save the time that it would cost him to put into the Port. I didna see anything wrang in him wanting to save time, and sae I agreed to meet him as he appointed. That was how it happened to be at night. Is that clear, Mr. Carnegie?"

"Quite clear, so far."

"Now then, ye want to ken why I should hae to gie him sic a heap o' siller. In a word then—because it was his ain. Although he's an awful man for whisky, Skipper Carrach has saved siller in my employ, for besides giein' him guid wages I favoured him on account o' his sister Girzie Todd, or Carrach as is her right name, though she changed it to Todd when her wean was born, to gar folk imagine that she had been a wedded woman. As she would never explain anything about it to anybody, folk were just left to think what they like, and in course o' time her ain name came to be forgotten, especially as she had been little ken'd at the Port afore she left my house to bide there."

As if overcome by the memory of that

event, he paused, wiped his nose hurriedly, and then deliberately laying the handkerchief across his knees to be ready for future use, he proceeded—

"But I minded; my repentance has been ower lang and sair to allow me to forget, Lord kens. I needna fash you wi' that, however. I just mention it to let you understand how it was I favoured Carrach sae muckle: it was for his sister's sake. He made siller, and I had it in keeping for him. He wanted to make mair, and as the worship o' Mammon tempts men who are no guided by Christian principle into wicked acts, it tempted him to the slave-trade, which he's been hankering after for the last twalmonth. My principles wouldna allow me to join him in such an inhuman traffic, and at last he resolved to enter it himself. So he bought the schooner *Ailsa*, for which I paid on his account, and he demanded the balance o' his siller. The balance amounted to a hunder pounds, and of course I agreed at once to pay him his due. But I was angry wi' him for breaking wi' me, and told him if he ever came back I would expose the nefarious trade he had been engaged in."

"Quite right too," muttered Mr. Carnegie.

"Maybe I did say that I would gie him ower to the hangman; but that was just a strong way o' expressing my indignation. Now ye ken why I met him on the Links last night and why I gied him the siller. Is it plain to ye, and is there anything else ye want to learn?"

All this appeared to be so straightforward, so much of it agreed with what Carrach himself told her, and with what she had heard Girzie say, that Jeanie, in spite of herself, felt her supporting hope tottering under her. And yet she did not doubt the truth of her convictions! The woman's faith in her husband still rose above all reason. The man might tremble at his own doubts of her; but her trust in him transcended, defied all proof and argument.

"Where is the paper ye were sae anxious

to get him to sign before a witness?" she said with teeth set.

The Laird wheeled round and laid his hand upon the desk as if about to produce the document on the spot; but, changing his mind, he faced her again.

"No, I will not show it to ye," he said stiffly; "it would do nae guid if your suspicion o' me is so strong as that comes to. But I will place it in the hands o' the fiscal the-day, and he'll let ye see it. Meanwhile, I may tell ye that it can gie ye sma' gratification, for it's nothing more than a receipt in full o' a' claims against me and mine. Is there anything else?"

He partly closed his eyes and folded his hands on his handkerchief, waiting in complacent resignation to hear what might be her next objection.

"If everything was sae fair between ye, why did ye allow him to force me awa' wi' him?"

"I beg ye to remember, Mistress Gray, that I protested against ony violence toward ye;

and you must be aware that for me to hae
attempted to fight wi' him for ye, would
hae been just to hae got mysel' hurt without helping you.   But to tell the truth,
ye didna seem to me to be so dreadful
anxious to win awa' from him as ye make
out now."

That was the first thing he had said—in-
sinuating and gross as it was—which gave
her hope that she might yet prove how
utterly false was his apparently plausible explanation.

"Ye saw me strive wi' him, ye heard me
cry for help, and yet ye haena even made
ony attempt to acquaint my friends wi' what
had befallen me."

That touched him; but only to the extent
of causing him to open his eyes quickly.

"It was a neglect, I admit," he responded,
taking a pinch, "but no intentional.   The
first thing I meant to do this morning was to
see your faither; but I hadna got half through
wi' my breakfast when Girzie came here like
a rampant idiot and drove everything clean

out o' my head till ye came yoursel'. Is there
onything else?"

He kept so near the line of truth that it
was difficult to mark at what points he
diverged.

"Mr. Carnegie," she said quietly, "would
you leave me a minute wi' the Laird?"

The lawyer looked at her doubtfully; but
something in the calm face, suggestive of a
purpose and of strength, decided him. He
rose immediately and quitted the room,
almost stumbling over Mrs. Begg, who had
been standing with her ear at the door.

The Laird's eyes blinked with some curiosity as he waited for the issue of this unexpected arrangement.

She stepped close up to him, looking fixedly
in his face; and she spoke in a low firm voice.

"What ye hae said looks sae like the truth
that it may cheat other folk, and will, nae
doubt; but it canna cheat me."

"Really, Mistress Gray, I dinna see your
meaning."

His voice had something of the harshness

in it Robin had noticed on the occasion of his last visit, when the Laird had been speaking to Mrs. Begg.

"I mean this: that the *Colin* was burnt by your orders; that Carrach is a murderer, if no by your orders at least through your schemes, and ye seek to shield him now at the cost o' an innocent man's life, to save yoursel' frae the harm his confession would do ye."

"You're a bauld woman, Mistress Gray" —(affecting indignation, but his thin lips trembling nevertheless).

"Ye shall find me sae, for day and night I'll follow ye frae this hour out until God pleases to do my man justice, in the eyes o' the world, whether he be dead or living."

"I'll take care to let the fiscal ken what ye say. Daft folk are no just left free to annoy decent and peaceable subjects as they may take it in their heads."

"Ye stand your ground weel, sir, but I'll gie ye ae chance yet. I ken it wasna your hand that struck the blow—ye couldna do that. Ye would torture a puir wretch wi' lees and shame, and ye would look on and smile, and maybe say a prayer ower his dead throes. But ye wouldna up wi' your hand to end his pain at ance. That would be ower muckle risk. But the guilt is on your shouthers for a' that, mair than on the shouthers o' a rough-witted chiel' like Carrach. If ye save yoursel' that's a' you care for. Weel, gie me the means o' saving my guidman, and I promise ye that I'll do naething till ye hae had time to win safe awa' frae the place."

A pause, a strange breathless stillness in the room, and then he said deliberately—

"As I'm no guilty, Mistress Gray, I hae nae need to bargain wi' ye for my life."

She turned away disheartened, but not beaten.

He followed her to the door, and, with a sigh and a considerate dab of his head in her direction, as if recommending her to the care of her friends, he took leave of Mr. Carnegie.

"Ye'll tell the fiscal should ye happen to

meet him that I want to see him particularly the-day," he said; "there maun be the fullest investigation into this business. I canna allow the aspersions Mistress Gray has cast on my character to go unnoticed, though they are ridiculous enough almost to confound themsel's. And by the by, as ye canna act for me in this matter, seeing that ye're on her side, would ye recommend me some trustworthy writer frae Ayr to look after my interests?"

The lawyer promised, and stepping into the gig, in which Jeanie was already seated, he drove away. He was dissatisfied, and looked steadily at the road before them, not speaking a word until they were within sight of the Port.

"I'm afraid you hae allowed your suspicions against the Laird to carry ye a wee thing ower far," he remarked, touching the horse with his whip unnecessarily. "I own there was suspicion, or I would not have been with ye the day; but there was no proof; and it's my opinion now that the way he represents the affair puts proof farther away from us than ever, although there's no saying what may turn up against Carrach."

She was a degree more disheartened by this, for it sounded to her somewhat like an intimation that he proposed forsaking her cause. But she only answered quietly—

"We'll see."

Mr. Carnegie was a worthy man; but he was threatened with the loss of an important client, and the Laird had been very plausible. He could not help doubting whether he had followed the wisest course for his own interests, notwithstanding his sincere desire to help Mrs. Gray.

CHAPTER VII.

A SACRIFICE.

"Content am I, if Heaven shall give
But happiness to thee—
And as wi' thee I'd wish to live,
For thee I'd bear to die."—*Burns.*

Hutcheson was lounging at the lawyer's door when the gig drove up.

"You're soon back," ejaculated Mr. Carnegie.

"Hae ye seen him?" cried Jeanie, reaching eagerly toward the man.

"I got word o' him sooner nor I expected, and that's how I'm so soon back."

"Hae ye seen him?" she repeated.

"Aye, mistress, I hae, and I'm looking for him here every minute."

"Where is he?"

"That I dinna ken. He just told me to say

he would be here as soon as he could get through wi' what he had to do."

"Are ye sure he'll come?"

"What would he no come for? The minute I acquainted him that it was you wha had sent for him, he bade me come back here and wait for him."

Mr. Carnegie took Jeanie into the little parlour where they had breakfasted, and left her there, whilst he disposed of various matters of business in his office. He promised that the moment Falcon arrived she should see him.

She had not very long to wait; but her feverish impatience made the minutes drag slowly. She had parted with him only a few days ago, bitterly praying that they might never meet again; and here she was burning with desire for his appearance. What an age of suffering she had passed through during those five days, and how far that night on which they had parted seemed to have receded! Measured by the anguish she had endured, those days were years. The period of happiness slips by, leaving only a faint trace behind in pleasant memories: but misery cuts deep tracks in our hearts, marking its slow and tortuous passage.

At length there were footsteps in the lobby. Mr. Carnegie's voice sounded with unusual distinctness, the door was opened, and a man entered.

Grainger!—and yet not Grainger, but James Falcon!

The only difference she could distinguish between the two was that this man's face was bare, and Grainger's had been half covered by a bushy beard. Everything else, the figure, the blue flannel shirt, the hat with its broad brim which had been always drawn so far over his brow, that together with what had seemed his sulky habit of sinking his chin on his breast, had prevented her forming any idea of the character of his features—all appeared to be the same as Grainger's. And yet the uncovered head and face she saw now were certainly Falcon's.

She had started up, on his entrance, but she

remained silent, staring at him in wonder. Was it possible that she had been several hours in his presence and yet had failed to recognize him? She could not understand that. But it was not so wonderful after all. She had been really very little near the man on board the schooner; he had spoken to her only in the briefest and gruffest manner; she had been all the time excited, with her mind fixed intently on one object—escape; and, most important, she had been under the impression that Falcon was dead. Under the circumstances, it was little marvel that she had failed to identify him.

He had halted near the door, and stood as if expecting her to speak; but, finding her dumb, he broke the silence himself.

"You sent for me, and I hae come, Mistress Gray, as I said I would, only when you yoursel' prayed me to come to you."

His voice was low and sad, but quite steady. It was the first time he had addressed her by her married name, and it sounded oddly in her ears. But it intimated with what resolute will he had set himself to recognize the barrier which had risen between them. How much he had suffered before he had taught himself to pronounce that name calmly she could guess from the slight hesitation of his tongue at the word, but a stranger would scarcely have noticed it.

That form of address reminded her of the serious work before her, and stirred her to action.

"I sent for ye, Jeames Falcon," she answered, and there was tenderness as well as firmness in her tone, "to ask ye to help me to save my guidman frae a death o' shame."

He made no response; his lips were closed tightly, and a faint spasm twitched his features.

She approached him, trembling with eager hope and fear, watching his face intently.

"Ye winna refuse me that, Jeamie?" she pleaded softly. "Ye winna refuse to satisfy Robin how muckle he has wranged baith you and me in his thoughts, by proving yoursel' his best friend in the hour o' his sair need?"

His head sunk further on his breast, and yet he made no reply.

"For my sake, Jeamie; for the sake o' a' I hae tholed on your account, and you on mine, dinna refuse me this last service."

He almost broke down at that, and he shaded his eyes with his hand whilst he spoke huskily—

"Me save him!—that's a hard job ye ask me to undertake, harder than ye seem to think. But a' your pity is for him; ye hae nane to spare for me, although I hae lost everything, and he has won what I hae lost. It's against nature for me to try to restore him to the happiness that his life bars me frae for ever—the happiness that I think him unworthy o', after the scorn he cast on you."

"Ah whisht, Jeamie, dinna speak that way. He was deceived by fause tongues and blinded wi' his passion. Dinna think o' that—only think that it's an innocent man in peril o' his life, and help me to save him. I ken that it's hard for you to help him, and my heart is as sair for ye as it is for him. I wouldna ask ye to do this, but that there's nae other body wha can help me as ye could if ye would."

"I did not mean to speak that way," he said, with an effort controlling his emotion. "I came to learn what ye sought wi' me, and to do your bidding if I could. You hae asked more than I thought I could ever do even for you, and that made me forget mysel'. But it's the last time you shall ever hear word frae me about what's gane and by. The lassie wha filled life wi' hope and light to me is dead; but for her sake, for sake o' the sweet memory she has left me, I will do what I can for you, even to helping Robin Gray in his need."

His voice was low and tremulous with emotion—pitiably sad to hear—in spite of the huge struggle of the brave fellow to render it calm and steady.

She bowed her head, her tears fell fast, and she could not speak for a while. She dried her eyes at length, and looked up.

" Thank ye, Mister Falcon."

And with that word, the last link which connected the man and woman who stood together in this room with the youth and maiden who had plighted troth at the door of the fisherman's cot—such a long weary time ago it seemed—was snapped. It cost them an acute pang, as if some vital chord of the heart or brain had broken. He started as if a pistol had exploded beside his ear when she called him Mr. Falcon.

The separation was complete; the past was really dead, and they were calmer afterward, abler to carry forward the work which duty demanded of them. Tears, regrets, and vain thoughts of what might have been, were all thrust from them from that hour. What tears they might shed in secret, what hidden regrets they might entertain, were those which are given to some loved one who now lies cold and silent in the grave. That was what they became sensible of when Jeanie said, "Thank ye, Mister Falcon."

"Will ye come into my office now?" said

Mr. Carnegie, appearing at the door; "there is nobody likely to interrupt us, and I want to make a note of whatever information you can give us."

Jeanie and Falcon followed him into the office. She sat down, he stood beside the desk, at which the lawyer seated himself pen in hand. Hutcheson sat on the corner of a little table by the window.

"The first thing we want to know then," proceeded Mr. Carnegie, "is how the poor lad Wattie Todd—for I suppose there can be no doubt that it's him?"

"There can be no doubt from what I have heard," answered Falcon.

"Just that. Well, the first thing we want to know is how he came to have on the clothes you had been seen wearing only two or three days previous?"

"On the Monday the Laird sent up a message for me to meet him at the second milestone on the Ayr road. It was early in the morning, but I started at once, and was at the place nearly an hour before he joined me.

He came in his gig. He told me that he was going to Ayr, and from something he had learned believed that he would see Carrach there. I was waiting at Askaig only for Carrach in order to learn what ship Hutcheson had sailed in from Liverpool. The Laird was to ask him, and he objected to me applying to you, sir, at once, on the score that if Carrach got the least hint of what I was wanting he would turn upon me and charge me with setting fire to the *Colin.* I did not fear that, but thought it better not to give him a chance of escaping me, and so agreed to the Laird's plan."

The lawyer ceased writing, frowned, bit the end of his quill, and looked dissatisfied.

"I went with him at once to Ayr. We remained in the town all day, the Laird leaving me for a couple of hours to make inquiries about Carrach, whilst he transacted some business with M'Laren & Sons, High Street. The business I have since learned was the purchase of the schooner *Ailsa.* I went to the inn where I had stopped on the day I landed from the south, and got a bundle containing a suit of clothes which I had left there in order to be able to walk the quicker home here. I didna then ken what was waiting for me, or I wouldna hae been in such haste to come back."

"Did you hear of Carrach?"

"No, I did not hear anything of him, and the Laird said we must wait a few days longer. I now believe that he had no expectation of seeing him there, and that he had taken me away from Askaig merely to prevent me meeting Cairnieford, who called during my absence."

Again Mr. Carnegie bit the end of his pen, and this time uttered a short "umph."

"The next morning—that was Tuesday morning you'll mind—I put on the clothes I had brought with me from Ayr and threw those I had been wearing aside. About ten o'clock Wattie Todd came up to me, poor lad. He had taken a great fancy for me, and I liked him. He was with me every day, and was my only comrade during the week I staid at Askaig. Rob Keith was so talkative that in the state of my mind at the time I could not endure him.

"Wattie and I went out as usual to the hills. We didna heed though it was raining, at least I didna heed, and Wattie made no complaint. He liked to be thought manly and fit for onything that onybody else was fit for. We went down by the burn and noticed that it was rising fast. I was going to pass under the Brownie's Bite when Wattie stopped me.

"'Dinna gang that gate, Jeamie,' he said, and I noticed then that he was shivering as if very cold.

"'Why no, Wattie?' I speired.

"'It's no lucky to cross the Brownie's teeth, ye ken, or he'd be sure to swallow ane o' us afore lang. Eh, man! what a big mou' he maun hae! He'd swallow the house if it was to tum'le ower. Come awa', let's gang up again.'

"It was the first time he had refused to follow me anywhere; indeed, he had always been so reckless in following me across the most dangerous passes that he had several times alarmed me, and rendered me more careful of the routes I chose for our wanderings. I went back with him to the house. He was still shivering. He was always cold like, poor lad, but seemed more so than usual on this day. I discovered that he was wet to the skin, and told him to take the clothes I had cast off and put them on. I was wet enough myself; but I did not care for that. I was indifferent to every discomfort.

"He was not quite willing to put on the clothes, but I got them for him and forced him to put them on—Lord forgie me, for I think that was the cause of his death. He took his clothes over to the barn and hung them up to dry. I went with him, and we lay down amongst some hay, covering ourselves for warmth. We talked. I could always talk with him, for he told me of all that had happened at the Port whilst I had been away. I fancied that the more I heard of it the more indifferent I would grow to-

wards the place and all its miserable associations. In return he would have me tell him
about ships and guns and fights, and that
pleased me too ; for whilst I spoke I fancied
that the thought of action would draw me
into it again, and thus enable me to forget so
much that I wished to forget.

"After dinner we went back to the barn.
The rain was falling heavier every minute,
the wind was rising, and we could hear the
spate gathering force. Wattie was frightened
when the thunder and lightning commenced,
and at last we went into the house. I found
Mistress Gray there."

He paused; he felt that he could not tell how
angrily she had blamed him for enticing her
there with a false message. She relieved him.

"And I accused ye o' trying to raise dis-
peace atween me and my guidman," she said
quietly. "I ken how wrang I was; I owned
to ye before ye left me that night that I ken'd
I was wrang. A' that passed frae that time
to the time ye quitted the house Mr. Carnegie has heard. But ye had better tell it

too that it may be written to satisfy Robin o' the truth o' what he was told."

Falcon briefly narrated what had passed, exactly as Jeanie had already done.

" From the moment I ran out of the house," he concluded, " I never saw Wattie Todd again. I heard him calling something after me, but the storm was too loud and my own excitement too great to let me hear what he said. The next morning I discovered that in my haste I had snatched up his bonnet instead of my own."

"Thank you, that's perfectly clear how he came to have on your clothes, and as he was much about your size, and as his features were unrecognizable, that explains how his body was mistaken for yours," commented the lawyer.

" And now tell us," said Jeanie, " how ye came to be on·board the *Ailsa* and calling yoursel' Grainger."

" Eh!" exclaimed Mr. Carnegie, " hae we found Grainger as well as Falcon?"

" Aye, it's even sae, or my e'en hae deceived me greatly."

"It is so," said Falcon, "and Hutcheson can corroborate what I say to the moment when I went on board the schooner. When I left Askaig I made straight for the Ayr road, never heeding the dangers o' the darkness and the storm. Besides, I was in a state which made danger welcome. But I got safe to Ayr a while before any of the inns were open. I had to wander about for several hours before there was anybody stirring to give me the information I wanted. At last I learned that a boat had sailed the day before, and there would not be another until the end of the week.

"I thought of starting by the coach, but it would not leave until next day, and then, so eager was I by any means in my power to put distance between me and Portlappoch, that wearied as I was I proposed to start on foot that afternoon for Carlisle. I was down at the quay when that resolution occurred to me, and I was just moving away when I met Hutcheson."

"That's right," commented Hutcheson,

nodding to add strength to his confirmation, and swinging his legs for the same purpose no doubt; "and pleased and astonished I was to see ye, when I had been thinking for a towmond past that ye was at the bottom o' the sea taking your dram wi' our friend Davy."

"We went up to the inn together, and whilst we drank, we of course spoke of the *Colin* and how his statement had been obtained from him."

"Oh, there was nae particular wark about it. Carrach just tauld me that he didna want to hae ony mair ado wi' me, and I needna waste time travelling back wi' him. I ken'd that my word would be nae weight against a' the others, and as a guid berth was offered me through Carrach on board the *Royal George* I just took it, and signed the paper he'd got drawn up by a snivelling lawyer body—nae offence to ye, Mr. Carnegie, he wasna like ye in ony respect."

"Thank you. What you say now is exactly the same as you told me this morning."

"Then you know about that," resumed Falcon; "and I need not give you the explanations which passed between us in detail. But when I told him that I had been waiting for Carrach, he informed me that he had seen Donald, who had been one of the *Colin's* men —the special friend of the skipper—and who had been unaccountably spiteful towards me. Hutcheson had spoken to him, and learned that he was then waiting for Carrach, who was to take command of the *Ailsa*, which had just been bought by the Laird.

"Till that moment I had been so eager to get away from the country that I had resigned all thought of punishing Carrach for his crime, and the many sorrows it had brought upon me and others. But fancy or hate put it into my head that Providence had placed the means of bringing this man to justice in my hands. I asked Hutcheson to help me, and he was ready with all his heart when I told him something of the mishaps which had befallen me through Carrach's villany. We waited for Carrach.

" Yesterday morning we saw him with Donald at the harbour change-house. I got near enough to hear what they were saying. Carrach was telling Donald that they were to lie off the Links, and the Laird was to signal to them that night. As the business was particular and private, he did not want to have more men on board than they could help. I had not suspected the Laird of being this man's accomplice until that moment. The suspicion once roused I remembered many incidents which had appeared to me singular when they occurred, but which were quite plain now. The Laird had been fooling me all the time, and was really trying to help Carrach to escape me, instead of helping me to lay hands on him.

" I determined to discover if possible to what extent the Laird was involved. I borrowed this suit of clothes from Hutcheson, and got my face covered with a beard by the barber at the cross, on the pretence that I wanted to surprise my friends who had not seen me for some time. I soon found Donald seeking hands; but hands were short for a long voyage, and I was the only man he could get who was ready to start that night. But he got three other men who agreed to ship next day.

"That was all I wanted, for the schooner required to lie off the harbour next day to ship her crew, and by that time I would have learned all I wanted to know. I gave Hutcheson the instructions which he has carried out, and I went on board the *Ailsa*. Neither Carrach nor Donald had the least suspicion of my real character. I affected to be surly, in order to keep them from speaking to me more than was necessary, lest in answering my voice should betray me. We anchored off the Links, and Carrach made me turn in and take a rest for a couple of hours, so that I might be fresh to relieve Donald.

"I suppose this was chiefly to prevent me seeing anything that might be done. I went below; but immediately crept up again and remained on the watch. Carrach and Donald lowered one of the boats; and about an hour afterward—in the midst of the skipper's impatient grumblings, which enabled me to understand that this meeting with the Laird was of much importance—a light signalled from the shore. He answered it, and then put off in the small boat.

"'When he came back, bringing Mistress Gray with him, I was alarmed for her sake and for my own, for I feared that she would detect my disguise, and in her surprise betray me. I went on deck just after they arrived. From some words I heard Carrach say to her I knew that she had been brought there by force; but I was puzzled by her quiet conduct. I grumbled loudly to the skipper, in order to give her some courage by showing her that one of the men on board was not entirely under his control."

"And it did that," broke in Jeanie gratefully.

"And also with the purpose of preparing her for the sound of my voice, so that it would either deceive her as I wished, or prevent her from showing too much surprise in the event of recognition. I wished to deceive her, because I had promised her that she would never see me again until she herself prayed me to come to her. I did not know then the sad reason she had for never expecting to see me again in this world, whether she wished it or not. When you" (turning to her) "spoke to me at the helm I understood your purpose in keeping so quiet, and I saw your distress at discovering that the boat had gone adrift. You thought me callous and unwilling to help ye, but it was because—weel, no matter; I am no to speak about that."

He paused. She looked him steadily in the face; and somehow the quiet trust in him which her eyes expressed gave him courage. He went on:—

"My purpose on board the *Ailsa* changed from the minute you set foot on deck. I had come there to find proof of the Laird's complicity with the Highlander. I was there then only to save you. I would have felled the man if he had touched you against your

will, and I nearly did it once, as you'll mind;
but I checked myself in time. It was an
unfair advantage I was taking, and besides I
wanted to deliver him as sound as possible to
the hangman. You know how I fastened
Donald in the forecastle and Carrach in the
hold. The only thing that I have to explain
now is why I left you so long locked up in
the cabin. There was no other reason than
that I was determined not to let you recognize me if I could help it. For the same
reason I left you as soon as we landed."

"And as he ken'd that I was to be here the-
day," added Hutcheson, "he was on the look-
out for me, and that's how I got word o' him
sooner than I expected."

Jeanie rose.

"Has the opinion ye expressed to me on
the road, Mr. Carnegie, been changed wi'
onything ye hae heard?" she asked.

Mr. Carnegie scratched his ear and bit the
end of his pen, coughing as he spoke.

"Opinions are no the thing, Mrs. Gray; it's
facts we want. There's plenty in what has

been said to form opinions on the subject; but so far as I can see there is not a grain of positive proof yet to connect the Laird with either of the crimes, and the one seems dependent on the other. There's the gold to be sure, but his explanation about that looks quite sound and natural."

She turned quietly to Falcon, drawing her plaid around her.

"Our work begins now," she said, "and while ye hae been speaking a notion has come to me o' where it should begin."

"Where?"

"Wi' finding the man wha brought the gig for me to gang to Askaig."

"The fiscal and myself have been trying to find him for the last two days and have failed," observed Mr. Carnegie, positive and somewhat nettled by her cool way of taking the matter out of his hands.

"But I think we may find him now."

"Aye, have ye minded who he was?"

"No, but I hae a suspicion o' wha he was."

"Whom do you suspect?"

She looked at Hutcheson.

"Was it no on Wednesday morning that you first met Donald at Ayr?"

"Aye, Wednesday morning."

"Ye're sure o' that?"

"I'll take my davy on't ony minute, for I only landed mysel' on the Tuesday, and it was the next morning I met him."

"Then I think it might hae been him," she said, glancing at the lawyer; "sae we'll gang to the lock-up, Mr. Falcon, and ye can question him about it."

"I ken something o' the chiel', sae I'll gae wi' ye," said Hutcheson.

"Mind what ye say to him," warningly ejaculated Mr. Carnegie: "you'll find me here when you're done."

CHAPTER VIII

TRACES.

"My hearth is growing cauld,
  And will be caulder still ;
And sair, sair in the fauld
  Will be the winter's chill."—*Thomas Smibert.*

The lock-up of the Port comprised the ground floor of a two-story house in the middle of the main street. The upper flat, to which access was obtained by a straight stone staircase built outside the wall, was occupied by the constable and his family. The entrance to the lower flat was by a dirty-looking door beneath the landing of the stair.

The interior of this primitive kind of prison was very simply arranged. There were white-washed stone walls, a stone floor with several ruts where the stone had been worn or chipped out; a form, a stool, and a high desk,

all of unpainted wood, but browned with age
and service and marked with cracks and
notches.   At the high desk Geordie Armstrong penned his despatches, on which, in
his estimation, the safety of the country de-
pended, and at the same time kept his eyes
on the two narrow doors of what were called
the cells.

The doors were made of stout oak, and had
withstood unshaken the furious batterings of
many a drunken clown who had been locked
up to bring him to his senses.   The cells
were really cells in point of size.   They were
not more than six feet by five inside, and
scarcely permitted a tall man to stretch himself on the floor.   They contained no furni-
ture beyond a bundle of straw thrown on the
floor for the prisoner to rest on if he chose.
They were lighted only by a slit cut in each
of the doors, which served also to enable the
constable to overlook the conduct of the
temporary occupants.

As Falcon and Jeanie, accompanied by the
some time mate of the *Colin*, entered the

lock-up, the door being open, they heard Geordie Armstrong's authoritative voice raised.

"I wish ye would let me finish my report, woman; I tell ye I canna let ye inside the cell wi' him, and if he winna answer ye through the door whatever ye want to speir ye maun just wait for the fiscal. The chiel' wha gied them in charge told me no to let onybody, no even the Laird o' Clashgirn himsel', in aside them."

"When will the fiscal be here? I hae waited hours and he hasna come yet."

"Weel, he's later nor he said he would be, but we servants o' justice canna just control our ain time. He'll be here sune, nae doubt."

The woman turned round a wild haggard face, which even Jeanie had much difficulty in recognizing as that of Girzie Todd. She had come straight from Clashgirn to the lock-up, and although Armstrong had persistently refused to admit her to Carrach's cell, he had permitted her to talk to him as much as she pleased through the wicket of the door.

She had been trying all this time to obtain from her brother some hint of the truth or falsehood of the charge laid against him. She told him who had been the victim, and that she believed another person guilty of the crime. But he had remained doggedly silent, only bidding her once or twice to "go away and mind her own pusiness."

She believed that if she could get in beside him he would tell her what she wished to know, but Geordie would not open the door.

"Oh, ye're come," she cried bitterly, "and ye as weel, Jeamie Falcon, it's braw times ye hae gien us and my laddie to die for ye. Maybe this thrawn dog will open the doors for ye, though he winna for me that hae the best right to ken the truth. Try him."

"Let her in," said Falcon, accompanying the order with such a significant nod that Geordie discovered something he had not thought of before, and instantly produced the key.

"Ye'll take the responsibility yoursel'," he paused to say.

"Certainly."

"That's enough. Come awa', Girzie, and ye'll see the inside o't; ye're the first that was anxious for the sight in my time."

She passed rapidly into the dark little chamber. The door closed; Falcon and Jeanie stepped up to it, and the constable remained beside them stiffly erect, but, like them, listening.

They heard her speaking in low hurried accents, conjuring him by every tie of kindred, by service she had rendered him, by everything he feared or hoped, to tell her so far as he knew how her bairn had met his death.

She was kneeling down, for he had seated himself on his bundle of straw with his back against the wall, and had made no movement of any kind at her entrance. The agonized entreaty of the mother appeared to have no more effect on his obdurate nature now that she was kneeling beside him than when she had been at the other side of the door.

She pleaded with all the terrible eloquence her great sorrow inspired, but with no avail. She swore to observe his confidence inviolable, swore to bring the true assassin to the gallows, even if he should be the dead bairn's own father, and at last she obtained this answer from him in his usual stolid hoarse tone—

"You said that Falcon was no dead? Then you'll no thocht that I would slew your poy? No—Pe-tam."

She tried again, but all her efforts only obtained this second speech from him.

"Could you'll no save your breath and get us some ouskie, for it is tam dry in this hole?"

She knocked at the door to be let out. She could make nothing of him, and she saw at length it was useless trying to make him speak. Neither prayers nor threats moved him in the least. She came forth with bent shoulders and head bowed, weak and aged as if years had passed over her in the last half hour. She moved slowly, almost tottered, to the door, and was going out when Falcon touched her arm.

"Girzie."

She turned her head as if with difficulty, and her sunken eyes rested on his face: they were utterly devoid of expression.

"Wattie was the only friend I had when I was in sair trouble," he said, neither voice nor eyes clear or steady. "God kens how gladly I would change places wi' him the-day if I could. Next to yoursel' I think he liked me best, and ye canna ken how bitterly I feel your loss, thinking that I am in some way partly to blame for't. Dinna blame me ower muckle in thinking o' him."

She looked at him a long while before speaking, as if his words reached her from a distance; and then, feebly—

"I'm no doitered, Jeamie, though I'm broken doon sair by this, and I blame nae-body but them wha thocht the foul thocht, and struck the foul blow that robbed me o' my bairn."

"They shall pay for't, dinna doubt that—they shall pay for't."

As if she had been touched by an electric current, her form rose erect and firm to its ordinary stature; but it was only for a second and she sunk again.

"Aye, but there's the sting o't," she moaned; "on the ae hand is my brither, on the other hand his faither. Oh, the curse has followed him frae his birth, and the sins o' his parents hae been visited on him, and on them through him."

"I'll go down to the house wi' ye," he said, not understanding her allusions perfectly; "ye'll be better after a rest."

"Aye, maybe sae, maybe sae, and aiblins it was better that it should be as it is, for he was a puir weak half-witted creature, that a' the world scorned and laughed at, and he would hae had a miserable time after I was gane. But oh, if I ken'd—if I ken'd"—(her teeth clenched, and passion stirring within her again)—"I would hae justice if I ken'd the truth—I would hae justice."

Her pace quickened as her wrath flashed into renewed life.

"Ye shall ken the truth before many hours pass," he said as they stopped at her door.

"Gie me hope o' that—gie me hope o' that," she said eagerly, her eyes glistening.

"I can give you certainty of it, but I cannot wait to explain enow."

"Come ben, come ben a minute, I want ye to do something for Wattie."

He obeyed that summons at once, eager as he was to return to the lock-up.

"He sha'na be buried at the expense o' Nicol McWhapple," she went on, in a proud hard voice. "I'll gie ye siller—his siller that I saved for him, and ye can arrange about a grave for him. I canna do't, and I want to haste awa' doon to him to watch ower him and be near him to the last."

She removed the stone which she had pointed out to Robin Gray at the back of the chimney as the hiding-place of her savings, and drew forth a thick woollen stocking, the colour of which was faded. It was fastened with a bit of tape, and, when she had untied that, she emptied out a little pile of silver and gold on the table.

"Take what may be needed—spend it a' on him if ye can. It's a' his, was got for him, and I'll never need it mair, nor him now. A new coffin and a new grave, he maun hae that, and there's his ain siller to buy them. There's mair yet, dinna be feared if ye think that's no enuch."

She emptied the stocking, and this time with the money—which amounted to about forty pounds in all—there rolled out a small packet of paper.

"Aye, the dead come to life the-day," she said, shoving the packet towards him; "that's yours—they're letters o' your mother's."

"My mother's!"

"Aye, I nursed her when she was dying at Clashgirn. She gied me thae, and tauld me to read them, and no to let onybody ken I had them, but to gie them to you if ever the day came you should need them."

"Why did ye not give them to me before?"
and he held the relics reverently in his
hands.

"I couldna read them, sae I just stapped
them into the first safe place I could find,
biding the day when ye would need them
and would speir for them as I expeckit. I
hope the day isna past. I just obeyed a
dying woman's will sae far's I could; but
there's nae use me keeping them ony langer
seeing that my ain time's no sae far aff."

He put the letters in his pocket to examine
them at the first moment he might be alone.

"You must put all this siller back, Girzie;
I have taken what is necessary, and if more
should be required I will come to you for it.
I must run back now to the lock-up. I'll
thank you another time for my poor mother's
legacy."

He hastened away, leaving the woman
seated before the table, her long bony arms
stretched out on either side of the hoard she
had striven so hard and pinched so much to
save. She stared at it in a dull stupor.

What sacrifices she had made for this, and now it was utterly worthless to her! She had never been able to understand why the minister called it pitiful dross. She understood now, when she found it could not give her one grain of comfort.

CHAPTER IX.

CLEARING.

"I hear the gentle rush of wings—
 I see the light of wandering stars,
And many a budding hope upsprings
 Glittering with gowden dots and bars."—*W. B. Sangster.*

Jeanie and the others were waiting for Falcon; and as soon as he rejoined them he asked Armstrong to get him a light. The constable procured a lantern, and taking it in his hand Falcon entered Donald's cell, leaving the door partly open, so that the others might easily hear all that was said.

The man was standing leaning against the wall, his head sunk sulkily on his breast. When the rays of the lantern fell on him he roused himself, facing his visitor fiercely.

"What am I kept here for?" he growled, "I'd like to ken that. I haena done onything wrang, and by——"

He checked himself, and the expression of savage wrath on his visage changed to one of terror. Falcon had raised the lantern so that the light fell on his own face, and it was the recognition of it which caused the prisoner's alarm.

"You ken me, I think, Donald," said Falcon coolly.

The man's lips moved, but he did not speak.

"We have not been the best of friends formerly," Falcon proceeded; "but we'll maybe make amends for that yet. I have come to help you out o' your scrape, if you're sensible enough to take help."

Donald began to recover himself; the voice was perfectly human, and dispelled the fright which the speaker's sudden appearance had created.

"I hae done naething to bring me into the scrape," he said surlily, "and I'd like to ken by whase orders I'm here."

"By mine, then, if it does ye any good to ken."

" Yours!—then ye're a dooms scoundrel, and as sune's I get the use o' my hands, I'll gie ye something to mind for't," he growled.

" Toots, man, keep your temper, or it'll be a long while before ye get the free use o' your hands again."

" What hae I done?"

" Maybe you did not think there was much harm in it at the time, but a' your trouble is just brought on ye by the lee ye told Cairnieford's wife when ye went for her with the gig on Tuesday last."

Donald turned his face sulkily away from the light.

" I ken naething about what ye say."

" O, aye, do ye."

" If I did it, it's nane o' your business."

" I'm thinking ye'll find it mair my business than ye would like to own. Just come out here."

Falcon pushed open the door and stepped out of the cell.

Donald saw that there were others outside,

and made no movement to follow, although he had been eager enough a moment before to get a breath of fresh air.

At a sign from Falcon, Geordie Armstrong strode into the cell, griped the prisoner by the collar, and dragged him out.

"That's the man," cried Jeanie, recognizing him instantly, and wondering that she had failed to do so when she had first seen him on board the *Ailsa*.

But he had been far from her thoughts at that time, and it was only when sitting in the lawyer's office trying to remember any peculiarity of the messenger whose falsehood had brought about so much misery, that certain movements of his body, the gruff tones of his voice, and his figure had gradually become associated in her mind with those of Carrach's accomplice on board the schooner. It was like the discovery of an object which the eye has registered, whilst the mind has been occupied with other things. Absent, she could not have described any of his features; but, her suspicion once directed towards him, she identified him without hesitation.

The man hung his head sulkily and abashed. The bold assumption of knowledge with which Falcon had addressed him, and Jeanie's recognition, convinced him that further denial was useless.

"I did nae mair nor I was bidden," he muttered uneasily; "and if harm cam' o't it wasna my fault."

"You had better make a clean breast of it," advised Falcon coolly. "Holding your tongue will not help Carrach, and will do yoursel' some harm. Speak out and you'll save your own hide."

"What is't ye want to ken?"

Jeanie was about to speak, but Falcon checked her with a motion of his hand.

"Where were you on Monday night?" he asked.

"I was at Clashgirn wi' the skipper, wha had got word frae the Laird to come late and tap at his window without letting onybody see us."

"Did you stay there all night?"

"Aye; I slept on the floor and the skipper on a big chair. We gaed awa' before the folk were asteer in the morning, and walked up by to Askaig, but we didna gang to the house."

"Did you hear any conversation between the Laird and Carrach?"

"Na; they gaed ben the house and talked in another room."

"Who instructed you as to what you were to do?"

"The Laird himsel' in the morning before we left the house. He tauld me what to say, and was particular to get me to say it exack as he direckit. He said there was nae harm in't; it was just a bit fun he wanted to hae wi' ye and Cairnieford. He gied the skipper and me baith plaids to put on, no to let us be ken'd; and he gied me a bonnet besides."

"Go on; tell everything. What did ye do when ye got as far as Askaig?"

"We hung about till afternoon, when, as had been arranged, a chiel' brocht the gig frae

Clashgirn to the ford. The skipper speired at him if he had been sent to seek Falcon, and he said aye. Syne the skipper took the reins frae him and told him he might go home. As soon as the chiel' was weel awa', I took the gig doon to Cairnieford, and delivered my errand as ye ken. I took Mistress Gray to Askaig and left her in the house, while I gaed awa', pretending to seek somebody to let us ken what had come o' her guidman.

"That was what I was told to do if there was naebody in the house. If Rab Keith had been there I was to send him awa' on a gowk's errand to seek the Laird. If ye had been there I was just to leave Mistress Gray wi' ye and drive awa' as fast as I could. I drove to the end of the loaning, where the skipper was waiting for me. He bade me drive on to Ayr and bide there for him; as he wanted to see the end o' the ploy he couldna gang wi' me. I ken'd weel enuch that though he let on that he just wanted to see the upshot o' the fun, he was anxious to see ye safe awa' frae the place. I did as I was bidden and drove on to Ayr, and that's a' I ken o' the matter, barring that when the skipper joined me, he told me that ye had fa'en ower the Brownie's Bite, and was drooned. So help me, Heaven, I hae spoken the truth to the best o' my belief."

" He told you that I was drooned ? When did he join ye?"

" On Thursday night. I mind the time quite weel, because he explained to me that we were to clear the *Ailsa* next day, and to come up by to the Links for instructions frae the Laird."

Further questioning only served to confirm this statement, and obtained no other information except that the skipper's intention to lie off the port of Ayr to complete the crew had been changed in consequence of having Mistress Gray on board, as he was afraid that by any accident she might escape him, or find means of communicating with the shore.

Falcon told him that if what he had said proved to be true, he had nothing to fear for his safety. Donald asseverated its truthfulness with an oath, and was locked up in his cell again to await the fiscal.

Jeanie's eyes were bright with hope and gratitude. The darkness through which she had been so wearily groping was clearing at last; and James Falcon's was the hand which had brought the light. She was glad of that and proud of it—proud to know that she had not loved an unworthy man. Robin would own his worthiness too; he would be forced to own it when he learned that he owed his life to the man whom he had cursed as his cruellest foe. It was a selfish feeling, perhaps, but now that his danger was passing away she could not help being gratified at the thought of how completely his suspicions and accusations would be confounded.

"The warst is by now, Jeamie," she said, resting her hand on his arm and looking in his face with sweet thankfulness. "Mister Carnegie canna say ony mair that there's nae direct proof against the Laird."

Falcon turned his face from her: he could

not yet look at it, and hear that low tender voice, without feeling his resolution disturbed. It was a bitter delight to him still to be near her under any conditions; and his heart rose in mutiny against the task he had undertaken for her sake; for every step he advanced brought him nearer to the moment when face and voice must fade from him for ever.

He could only steady himself by taking the bit between his teeth, as it were, and hurrying on with the work of self-immolation: every pause was full of pain.

"I hope the worst is by," he answered, clearing his throat; "but Robin Gray will not be safe until we hae some evidence as to who struck Wattie Todd. As yet we can only prove that Carrach was at Askaig *during the day;* the crime was committed at night."

"But what we ken now will force the Laird to speak?"—(anxiously).

"He'll say nothing as long as it's possible to avoid it. But you go down wi' Hutcheson to Mr. Carnegie and tell him about

Donald. I'll join you in half an hour. I must go now and arrange about the burial of Wattie, as I promised Girzie. The fiscal will maybe hae come by that time, and after I see him we'll ken what to do next."

Falcon went up the street to the wright's. The wright was the undertaker of the town as well as the carpenter. He was not in the house at the time, but one of his children ran off to seek him. Whilst Falcon waited he took out the packet of his mother's letters Girzie had given him, and opened it, with the memory of a pale sad face rising out of the long-ago to soften the bitterness of the present.

Jeanie, on entering the lawyer's office, found herself in the presence of the fiscal and the Laird. The latter started at sight of Hutcheson, but recovered himself immediately, and said, in his sleek pawky way, that he was " very glad to see him looking sae weel after his long voyage."

The fiscal greeted Jeanie with one of his cheery smiles.

"The very person I was wanting to see," he exclaimed; "come away, Mistress Gray, and look at this."

It was a paper he had in his hand, which he extended to her. At first she thought it was the paper which she had signed as a witness to Carrach's mark. In size and fold it was exactly similar; but there did not appear to be so much writing on it as she had observed on the other at the moment of signing it.

" Examine it closely, if you please, and tell me if that is your signature," the fiscal continued, " I have had some conversation with the Laird, and it seems you lay much stress on the production of this paper, although I cannot see how it will help you, for it is nothing more than an ordinary form of receipt."

" That's no the paper I signed," said Jeanie calmly, handing it back to the fiscal.

The Laird at that dabbed his head forward, smiled benignantly, and took a pinch of snuff with the emphasis of a man who resigns all hope of convincing a stubborn opponent.

"Not the paper," said the fiscal, without the least surprise, "how do you make that out? I have compared the signature with the one on your deposition, and another Mr. Carnegie has got, and they seem to me the same."

"Aye, the writing is like enough mine to cheat mysel' almost. But when I was signing the paper that I mean, I noticed there was a heap o' writing on't, and besides I noticed Carrach's mark. The pen had slipped wi' him in making his cross, and there were twa wee spots o' ink just above it."

The fiscal darted a side glance at the Laird, smiling all the while. The Laird took another pinch of snuff with the former emphasis.

"I can do nae mair, Mister Smart," he exclaimed meekly, "ye'll just hae to do what ye think best. Ye will admit that I hae done everything in my power to assist the inquiry."

"Certainly, certainly," responded the fiscal, in quite a friendly tone, and that decided Jeanie to say nothing about Donald's confession so long as the Laird was there to distort it by one of his plausible explanations.

" Then ye dinna think it necessary" (smiling mildly at his own joke) " to put me in chains yet?"

" I cannot see the chance of that ever becoming necessary."

Clearly the Laird had satisfied the fiscal as well as the lawyer, that the suspicions raised against him by the wife of the alleged criminal were groundless. He had been about to leave when Jeanie arrived, and he had stopped to learn the result of her examination of the receipt. He now bade them all good afternoon in the most kindly spirit, and departed.

He got his pony at the inn, and rode homeward with a much longer face than usual, and with much more speed as soon as he had got clear of the Port. Somehow that threat Jeanie had spoken when he had felt himself so secure from discovery was haunting him—" Day and night I'll follow ye frae this hour out until God pleases to do my man justice."

That was what she had said, and the words had clung to his memory with curious distinctness. In spite of himself, his mind repeated them again and again as he rode homeward in the rapidly darkening winter gloaming.

The Laird had barely quitted the lawyer's office, when Falcon entered it with singular excitement in his voice and manner. He addressed himself abruptly to Mr. Carnegie, without appearing to notice the presence of others.

" Did you know Hugh Sutherland ?"

The lawyer opened his eyes at this sudden recalling of a man who had been dead nearly sixteen or seventeen years, and who had been away from the place six years or more previously.

" Do you mean the former laird of Clashgirn ?"

" Yes—him."

"To be sure I ken'd him, but that's about twenty-five years syne. What about that?"

"Would you know his handwriting?"

"I could not say, it's such a long while since I saw it. But there was some correspondence between us regarding the case of Sutherland *versus* Johnstone, which was a question as to the miller's right to draw water from the burn above Cairnieford. As the case was one of great importance, I preserved all the documents, and among them letters I received from Mr. Sutherland whilst I was in Edinburgh, and before he joined me there."

"Have you got them now?"

"Yes—somewhere" (looking vaguely round the office, and at various deed-boxes).

"Look them out, they'll be needed."

He turned to Jeanie, and catching her hand he pressed it tightly.

"I think the means to force the truth from the Laird are in my hands now," he said agitatedly; "wait here till I come back, and if you, sir" (to the fiscal) "can be here three hours from this, I'll have some important information to give you, I expect. I want you to come with me, Hutcheson."

"I will be here at the time you mention," said the fiscal; "I have plenty to occupy me till then. But where are you going in such haste?"

"To seek McWhapple."

"You'll find him at home, I believe."

CHAPTER X.

REYNARD UNEARTHED.

"Mesh'd in the net himself had twined,
  What subterfuge could Denzil find?
  He told me with reluctant sigh
  That hidden here the tokens lie."—*Scott.*

The candles were lit in the Laird's room, and a bright fire imparted a warm glow of comfort to everything around. The Laird himself was seated in his big chair busy with a book of accounts. Whatever nervousness he might have displayed when he first learned that he was suspected of complicity with Carrach, he was now as calm and methodical as when he felt his respectability most impregnable, and his yellow visage with the pale blinking eyes was as expressionless.

The door was rudely pushed open without warning and Falcon entered. He was flushed

with rapid walking, and his eyes were glistening with unabated excitement, although he
was making violent efforts to control it.

The Laird looked up quietly, and, observing who had made this unceremonious entrance, methodically closed his account book,
wiped his pen, and spoke—

"Od, it's extraordinar'! I didna expect
the pleasure o' seeing you. A fine habble you
hae brought us a' into."

Falcon had closed the door, and he stepped
up to the table opposite the Laird. The
latter leaned back on his chair, clasping his
hands before him, and blinkingly, but un-
moved, meeting the penetrating gaze fixed
on him.

"You're no looking weel," observed the
Laird complacently as the other did not
speak, "and you seem out o' breath. Will
you hae a dram?"

This equanimity irritated him; but he was
determined not to lose command of his temper, and so he answered decisively and with
forced calmness—

"I require nothing, thank you, but your close attention to what I have to say."

"Ye'll get that; but ye may as weel sit down."

Falcon, instead of accepting the invitation, looked at the man, amazed and puzzled that he could remain apparently so completely undisturbed when ruin and the gallows were at his elbow. He drew a long breath, renouncing all attempt to solve the problem at that moment, and proceeded abruptly—

" Have you made up your mind what to do about Cairnieford? Are you to speak out what you know and save him, or are you to hold your tongue and let him take his chance? That's the first thing I want to know."

" Od, it's extraordinar'!"—(with a mild expression of amused astonishment). " You're on that tack too. Weel, I would hae thought that you wouldna hae been sorry to find Mistress Gray a widow."

" No matter what you thought, and extraordinary as it may seem to you"—(growing firmer and more self-possessed as he proceeded)—"I mean to help him out of his scrape, and I mean you to give me the power to do so."

"Really? Do ye think I carry his free pardon in my pouch?"

"You carry it in your knowledge of what Carrach has done and what you directed him to do."

"Would a wheen auld bills o' lading and maybe an auld log or twa be ony use to ye?"

"You are disposed to treat the matter lightly, sir, but you will find it serious enough before it ends."

"To my thinking it's serious enough enow to thae wha are interested—I'm no."

"You will be when I tell you that Donald has confessed."

The Laird's head dabbed quickly forward, and immediately he leaned back again, smiling meekly; but the thin lips were not quite so firm as they had been. Evidently he had forgotten Donald, or he would have anticipated the danger and been prepared for it.

"Weel, what has he confessed?"—(quietly)
—"that he saw me ding the lad ower the
Bite?"

"He has confessed enough to implicate you
to such an extent that it will not be easy for
you to clear yourself."

"We'll see about that when we ken what
he's got to say against me."

"You know very well what he has got to
say about you; and now answer my question
—are you to speak before it is too late and
save Cairnieford?"

"Once for all then, I have nothing to say
that will help him."

And he took a pinch of snuff with the emphatic air of a man who declines to say a
word more on any consideration.

"You are determined not to help him?"

"Quite."

"I hope you will change your mind"—
(drawing out the packet of his mother's
letters).

"Ah, you're a young man yet, and sae
you're confident"—(with a species of benig-

nant pity for his inexperience). "Why, man,
if I ken'd o' onything that could help him
and wouldna hurt me, do ye think I wouldna
hae told it at once? And if, on the other
hand, I ken'd onything that the telling o'
would hurt mysel', do ye think me likely to
tell it so long as I could hide it? It's against
nature to think so."

"I never thought you would tell anything
so long as you could hide it; I have too
strong a proof in my hand of your hiding
capabilities to imagine that. But when a
man is likely to be stripped of every penny
he possesses, and to be hung into the bargain,
I think it is probable that he would be disposed to save his neck, and obtain the means
of living quietly in some remote corner, if he
could do so by speaking the truth for once
in his life."

"I have always admired the truth; and
have no doubt a man placed as ye suppose
would act so. But that's no my case, thank
guidness."

"That is exactly your case."

"Aye? I would be glad to ken how you make that out?"

"I must begin then by referring to the event which placed me under your care."

This time the Laird almost started to his feet, but again checked himself, leaned back, reclasping his hands and smiling feebly, while his complexion became sallower than Falcon had ever seen it, except on one occasion when he had been an invalid for several weeks.

"That's an event I hae reason to be proud o', so far as I am concerned," said the Laird in his martyr voice; "though I scarcely think you hae conducted yoursel' toward me in a way to make it pleasant for ye to mention the benefits I conferred on you and your mother. Puir woman, she was in sair need o' a friend when she found me."

Falcon found it difficult to restrain his temper at this patronizing speech; but he just paused a moment, and the thought of Jeanie helped him.

"You have many a time reminded me of the benefits you conferred on us, and no doubt

I ought to have been exceedingly grateful—
and I was, Heaven knows, until your eternal
boastings of your own goodness rendered
yourself and my gratitude alike contemptible."

"I'll no say a word about you, but you
were ay a thrawart lad; and onything I said
or did was just to imbue ye wi' a proper
Christian spirit."

"Your efforts seemed to me to lie rather
in the way of exalting your own charity. You
made me feel that so much that on one occasion—it was when you refused to let me have
Askaig—I reminded you that there were folk
who said you had other reasons than those of
charity for helping me and my mother."

"Folk say queer things in this world,
Jeamie"—(with a sigh).

"But the queer things they hinted at in
this case were true."

"Do ye think sae?" (the eyes blinking at
him curiously).

"I know it."

"Maybe ye'll let me know it too, then?"

"That is what I am here for"—(opening one

of the letters). "You became factor to Mr. Hugh Sutherland, the proprietor of Clashgirn, five years before he quitted the country."

"Quite true, and I had ken'd him a while before that."

"During the year in which he left home, you introduced him to an Irish gentleman, who was reported to be on a visit to some friends at Ayr. His real name was O'Coighly, although you called him Captain Jones. The captain invited Mr. Sutherland to meet him at his friends' house, and when Mr. Sutherland went to the house in Ayr he met six other men. He then discovered that they were members of what was called a sub-committee of a secret society, known as the United Scotsmen, which was in connection with another secret society called the United Irishmen. The objects of both were the overthrow of the government and the establishment of a republic."

"Aye, aye!" exclaimed the Laird, with affected interest, but moving his chair uncomfortably.

"Mr. Sutherland was much alarmed to find himself in such company, and afterwards forbade Captain Jones, or O'Coighly, to come to Clashgirn. Soon after that various persons were seized by the government and convicted of sedition. Mr. Sutherland, being naturally a timid man, was alarmed by these trials, and you took advantage of his terror to represent to him that a criminal information had been laid against him, and persuaded him to save his property by assigning it over to you and to save himself by flight to France."

"I told him nothing but the truth."

"I need not repeat to you the numerous pretexts by which you kept him from returning to his native country. At last he begun to suspect the trick which had been played upon him. You had, under the pretence of bad harvests and failing tenants, so reduced your remittances to him that you barely left him enough to live upon. In several of your letters you admitted that the transfer of the estate to you was only a trick; but at the end, when he threatened you with his immediate return, you set him at defiance by telling him to come and see what court would accept his explanation, that, to save himself from the consequences of his connection with the seditious society of United Scotsmen, he had made over his property to you."

" I never wrote that" (nervously).

" Further, you told him that the estate was yours," Falcon went on, " and that he would have to take it from you by the power of the law if he could. You knew the man you were dealing with; you knew that he would never have courage to take the matter into court, and you trusted that he had no friend with sufficient influence over him to persuade him to come boldly forward and trust to the justice of our laws to restore his property. He had such a friend, however, in the person of an Irish exile, named Dornay, who, with his only relative, a daughter, was living in the same house in which Mr. Sutherland lodged. Under Dornay's direction he proceeded to draw up a statement of the case; but before it was completed Dornay died.

" Mr. Sutherland soon afterwards married his late friend's daughter, and for five years was always proposing to carry out the plan suggested by his friend; but his resolution was too weak to permit him to take the necessary steps. Meanwhile his wife had a son—"

" If ye mean Miss Dornay as his wife, I'm in a position to say they were never married."

" His wife had a son," repeated Falcon with clenched teeth, "and when that son was five years old, Mr. Sutherland died, bequeathing to his wife your letters and his own statement of the case duly signed and witnessed. You sent Mrs. Sutherland money, and condoled with her in such a manner, that the friendless wife, believing the hypocritical professions of friendship and regret you made, gathered what little money she could, and, although weak and ill at the time, and wholly unfit for such a journey, came here with her child. She hoped that when she saw you she would be able to persuade you to restore to her son the property out of

which you had cheated his father, without
the necessity of legal proceedings.   She was
eager to try the experiment, more especially
because she had not the means of meeting
even the preliminary expenses of taking the
matter into court.

"She arrived here almost penniless, ill,
fatigued, and dying.   You saw her condition,
and you speculated on her death.   You knew
that if she had gone away from this house
your tenure of Clashgirn would have been
brought to a speedy end.   With the cunning
and hypocrisy which have enabled you to
succeed in so many things, and to blind the
eyes of honest men as to your real character
for so long, you received her into the house.
Pretending that you were not sure whether
or not it would be quite safe for herself or
her child to be known under their proper
names, you persuaded her to assume the name
of Falcon for a few days.   Your apparent
readiness to serve her blinded her, and she
consented.

"You had her conveyed to a bed, and she

never rose again. During the six days of her illness you called in no doctor, and you permitted only one person to see her besides yourself. You no doubt calculated that you could trust to that person's fidelity to your interests if occasion demanded the trust. Mrs. Sutherland, however, was completely deceived by you almost to the day of her death; but then her eyes became clearer. Without your knowledge she obtained pen and ink. She added to her husband's statement an account of your conduct to her, and folded it up with your letters and other documents which she had brought with her from France. She gave the packet to the woman who nursed her, and who had shown herself friendly, telling her to read the contents and give the packet to her son whenever he might require them.

"Mrs. Sutherland died. You buried her as Mrs. Falcon, the unfortunate wife of an unfortunate gentleman whom you had once slightly known; and out of charity you brought up her son as your drudge and de-

pendant. You made a good deal of capital
out of that act of benevolence; but I think
you have been a little too cunning for yourself in some respects. There were a few
people who suspected the truth, and did not
hesitate to say so. Not very long ago I
refused to listen to their suspicions, because
I thought even listening to them was ingratitude to you. Now I know their suspicions to have been true. That packet, which
my dying mother intrusted to her nurse, was
delivered to me to-day—this is it in my hand.
I have repeated these facts to satisfy you that
it is no empty threat I make in telling you
that I hold the power to ruin you, perhaps
to hang you."

The Laird had made numerous attempts
to interrupt this recital: he had shown be-
nignant pity for the speaker; then indignation; then injured innocence graduating back
to indignation. But Falcon, with pitiless
and stern aspect, had gone on, compelling
him to hear. The eyes of the Laird seemed
to sink as he listened, and the blue lines

beneath them deepened in hue, while the visage became of a sickly yellow complexion.

"Oom—hoo," exclaimed the Laird slowly, when Falcon at length paused: "and wha was't gied ye thae interesting papers?"

"Girzie Todd."

The Laird, with a sharp little cry, and an extraordinary agility, sprung from his chair and clutched at the documents Falcon was holding in his hand. But they were withdrawn from his reach in time; he was pushed back, and he stood, his shrivelled body quivering with baffled rage, and his eyes glaring and blinking at his own accuser.

There was no hypocrisy now; for once in his life Nicol McWhapple stood uncovered. He struggled hard to regain his self-possession, and a species of petulant venom obtained the place of his blind fury. He laughed shrilly as he gasped—

"I was—just making fun—when I pretended that I wanted to snatch the papers frae ye. What do ye come here to me wi' this story for? If ye think it's true, and ye can prove it, why do ye no gang to a lawyer at once and set the beagles at my heels?"

And he laughed shrilly again, his fingers moving nervously, and his eyes hungrily watching Falcon's hand.

"I'll tell you why I come to you before placing the matter in the hands of the authorities. Had you given me Askaig when I asked for it, you would have been safe to-day. As it is, your infernal trickery has so marred the dearest hopes of my life that I do not care a single straw for the wealth or position it is in my power to claim."

"Very kind o' you that."

"I come to make a bargain wi' you for Jeanie's sake. Clear Cairnieford of the false charge against him: and on the day on which he leaves the jail a free and unblemished man, I will deliver these papers to you to do with them as you please. I will leave the country, and you will never hear anything more of me or the *Colin.* Hutcheson has agreed to go with me; and you will be left to enjoy your fortune, if you can, without any fear, as far as I am concerned."

The Laird regarded him with a curious expression of wonder, suspicion, and spleen. It passed his comprehension that a man believing himself entitled to a fortune, and believing that he held the proofs necessary to obtain it, should willingly throw his chance away to rescue a man whom, according to the Laird's code, he should have been pleased to see removed from his way. His features curled into a sour sneer.

"Ye're unco generous at other folk's expense," he said presently; "bide a wee and I'll gie ye my answer to your proposition."

He limped over to the door, looked out to see that the lobby was clear, closed the door again, and faced Falcon with a mocking look.

"We're by oursel's, and for ony use ye may make o' what I say, it's just my word against yours; and I'll trust to my respectability, that I hae devoted my life to earn, to weigh the scale down on my side. So, I can

permit mysel' the pleasure o' speaking my
mind freely for once."

"It will be a treat, no doubt," rejoined
Falcon, coolly, and placing the packet of
papers in his pocket, he waited to know
whether his terms were accepted or rejected.
He could not guess the decision by any
symptom in the girning politeness with
which the Laird had now succeeded in cloak-
ing his nervous fury.

CHAPTER XI.

REYNARD RUN HOME.

" The cat has clomb to the eagle's nest,
    And suckit the eggs and scar'd the dame;
  The lordly lair is daubed wi' hair,
    But the thief maun strap an' the hawk come hame."—*Anon.*

"I have mentioned to you," began the Laird with a species of spiteful deliberation, "that I always admired the truth"—(Falcon smiled grimly);—"ye think that funny, but it's a fact for a' that, and I'll tell ye why. It has been a principle o' mine never to deny the 'truth, because I always found that I could twist its conclusions to my ain ends wi' far mair ease and far mair safety than it would hae been possible to do by telling lies. For the last twenty-five years I never told a lie that could possibly be avoided; and, consequently, folk finding so many things I said to be true, gied me credit for the rest. On that principle I'm gaun to own the truth to you now, although when it comes to other ears I will own it with the necessary modifications for my purpose. But wi' only you to hear me, and only you to bear witness against me, ye shall hae the whole truth, unqualified."

"Thank you."

"To begin then: all you hae said about Hugh Sutherland and about his wife and his bairn—that's yoursel'—is quite correct. All you hae said about me is quite true; and all you hae said about Carrach, and about my knowledge o' what he has done, is quite true. Is that no frank?"

"Exceedingly so."

"Od, man, ye hae nae idea what a straight-forward chiel' I am in my dealings. Ye hae ken'd me as the Laird, a kirk-going man with plenty o' siller; respected by maist folk and treated wi' civility even by them that didna like me and were ay ready to speak ill o' me ahint my back. But I was prosperous, and that made them mum afore my face. I'll tell ye what I was: a puir ragged bare-

foot bairn, motherless, fatherless, and friendless; lame, and no fit for hard work. A
tailor-body took pity on me and begun to
learn me his trade: and at the same time he
learned me to read and write. That let me
see the way to something better nor a tailor's
broad."

"You made good use of his lessons"—
(drily).

"I did that. I had been dunted about by
nearly everybody, and I saw that to be weakly
and puir was to be a football for whaever
was strong or rich; and I saw that the ae
thing everybody respected and bowed down
to, whether the owner was weak or strong,
was siller. I couldna alter my body or put
pith into it; but I made up my mind to
make siller. I got to be a clerk in a writer's
office, and there I met Sutherland. He was
a weak-headed, faint-hearted creature, wha
had quarrelled wi' every friend he had in the
world. I became his friend, and became his
heir exactly in the way ye hae stated."

The mocking coolness, and the degree of

unction with which the man confessed his villany, rendered it difficult for Falcon to remain quiet. He ground his teeth, determined to listen to the end.

"I'm a great villain ye would say," proceeded the Laird, observing the fierce movement of his hearer's features, and the effort by which an exclamation of anger had been checked; "say it out if it will do you any guid; there's naebody to hear ye but me, and that's neither here nor there. Weel, I became master o' Clashgirn: it cost me a heap o' wark to gain that, and it has cost me twenty years o' constant watching and contriving to make my position sure. After a' that, do you think that because ye come to me wi' a wheen papers ye hae gotten frae an auld wife, that I'm gaun to cower down before ye and do just whatever ye like to bid me?"

"You own that you have dreaded exposure, and in two hours the exposure will be made, unless you place in my hands now the means to save Cairnieford."

"I do fear exposure, and I would accept

your terms maybe, if it werena that it would just be louping out o' the frying-pan into the fire. Ane can endure the pan longest, and sae I'll bide in the pan."

"I offer you safety——"

"No, you offer me a chance of twa roads to ruin, and I prefer the longest. I can snap my thumb at your papers, onyway I can repudiate them, and I hae siller enough to carry the case frae ae law court to another until body and soul o' ye are worn out. But I canna do that wi' Carrach. So long as I say nothing about him, ye'll never get a cheep out o' him; for he'll ay be counting on me clearing him. But if I speak, he'll speak too."

"Then you admit that you are both involved in poor Wattie's death?"

"Od, man, I'm admitting everything, seeing we're by oursel's, so you can believe me that there was nae thought o' violence on our part, and there would hae been nane if it hadna been for a mistake. I never believed in violence mysel', for I could ay manage far better without it: if I thought o' ony in this case it was between you and Cairnie-ford."

"What had he or I, or the poor woman whose life you have made miserable, done to you, that you should have wiled us into this fiendish snare?"

"Ye want to ken that? I'll tell ye"——(venomously). "On the night you and me had some words about Askaig, you bragged to me that ye ken'd enough to hang me if ye liked to follow up the clue. Ye referred to what you had discovered o' our cheating the gaugers wi' the tobacco and brandy, and maybe ye had a notion o' Sutherland's case. It didna matter to me which; I never forgot your words. So I doubled the insurance on the *Colin*, and I told Carrach never to bring her hame again. I didna tell him to murder you—that might hae been done long syne when ye were a bairn if I had been disposed to violence. I just told him that I wouldna be sorry if you never came hame ony mair than the brig."

"And for that reason, I suppose, you worked your spite upon me when I returned?"

"I hoped that you had been drowned, but I wouldna hae sought to harm ye when ye came back if ye had gone away again as I advised. Instead o' that you threatened me —although ye didna ken o't at the time—wi' mair power on your side than ye had got before ye left. I feared that ye would meet Cairnieford and that he would help ye. He ay doubted me; he was the boldest of any who declared their doubts o' my dealings wi' Sutherland, and the first to suspect that Mrs. Falcon was naebody but Sutherland's wife. But on that score they had naething but suspicions, whilst I held proofs o' the upright character o' my transactions."

"You mean forgeries and lies as your proofs."

"That doesna matter. I wanted to get you out o' the country, and to prevent you meeting Cairnieford as a friend. The easiest way seemed to me just to make him suspicious o' his wife and you. If ye quarrelled and ane o' ye got killed, so much the better for me. But at the least there would be nae chance o' friendly dealings atween ye, and one or other would be sure to quit the country—I didna care which, but I had nae doubt it would be you. The plan was a braw ane, and would hae wrought about exactly as I calculated, if it hadna been for the blundering o' that stupid brute Carrach, wha wasna content to leave the scheme to work out its ain end, but maun bide to see the upshot o't, and sae spoil everything. Would to Heaven I had never seen him."

"You dislike the man, and yet would screen him from the punishment he deserves."

" Dislike him! I do that wi' a' my heart, but I hae a strong liking for mysel'. I would be glad to get rid o' him, and when we parted last night I thought I was never to see him again. I had arranged things sae that had he been awa' for a week he would never hae daured to show himsel' in this country ony mair. I'll tell ye how: He told me a' that took place at Askaig, and I wrote

it down as his confession. I got his mark to
it and Jeanie Gray's signature. In a week I
would hae given that paper to the fiscal as
though it had been sent to me privately.
The fiscal would hae acted on it, and I would
hae sent Carrach word, sae that to save his
neck he would hae ta'en guid care to keep as
far frae Portlappoch as the sea and his
schooner would let him."

" Where is that paper?"—(eagerly).

" In a safe place o' hiding, where neither
you nor onybody will find it without my
help. Had it no been for you I would hae
been safe and weel the-day. But ye hae been
like a stane round my neck frae the first day
I saw ye. Every day and every hour ye reminded me o' what was gane and by, and
kept me in tortures o' fear for what might
be to come; and now ye hae upset a' my
schemes, and ye shake the terror o' the gallows
in my face."

" I offer ye the means to escape it."

" Ye canna do that, and if ye could, I
wouldna accept it frae ye"—(with quivering

venomous passion)—"no, I'll stand my ground to the last now, for I may as weel die as lose everything I hae spent my life to win. I hae been frank wi' ye, I hae told ye everything, I hope ye're satisfied."

· "I am satisfied that the gallows is too mild a retribution for such as you."

"I'm glad ye're satisfied. Do ye ken why I hae told ye this? To let ye feel that you, a strong brawny chiel', are powerless before a weak lame auld man like me. I snap my thumb at your papers and at everything ye can say or do. I trust to my respectability, and I defy ye to do your worst. Now ye can go."

Falcon made a passionate movement as if about to obey his impulse and grip the wretch by the neck to drag him at once before the fiscal. But the deliberate defiance, pronounced with all the hissing spite of a serpent, checked him.

"You have chosen your course," he cried fiercely, his passion and loathing rendering articulation difficult, "and you will find it a short one; for, by Heaven, in three hours from this I'll give Carrach a companion. You need not think to escape me. Hutcheson is here, and he will take care of you until I return."

"I hae nae intention to quit the house."

Falcon, frowning, pulled his bonnet tight over his brow; the Laird's eyes blinked, his head dabbed, and he took a pinch of snuff, snapping the lid of the box with apparent confidence and satisfaction, then he bowed mockingly as he opened the door for his visitor. At the same time the outer door was loudly slammed to and locked; and, before Falcon could cross the floor, Girzie Todd stood on the threshold.

She had a wild haggard look, and her hands worked nervously. The kerchief which was fastened over her head had fallen back, and her thin iron-gray hair was straggling over her brow. She was panting as if she had been walking a distance rapidly. Her eyes had a vacant expression until they rested on the Laird.

He had been observing her in mute wonder, and now when she griped his arm he uttered a slight ejaculation of fright.

"Ye're a puir weak creatur'," she gasped in a hoarse undertone, "and ye hae brocht it a' on yoursel'."

"A' what—are ye gyte, woman? What's wrang?" he shrieked cowering.

"No, I canna let them tak' ye, muckle wrang as ye hae done me. Ye were the father o' my bairn, and I canna, canna for dead Wattie's sake, let them hang his father on the gallows if I can save him. Come awa', there's maybe time yet."

"What are ye raving about, woman? What do ye mean?"

She regarded him vaguely for an instant as if not quite understanding his question. Then, sharply—

"I mean that Mistress Begg has gien the fiscal a paper that she saw ye hiding aneath the big stane at the door. She took it out as soon as ye left the house, and it tells how my Wattie was done to death, and, O Lord,

O Lord, it was by my ain brother's hand and through your ill schemes."

Sobs choked her and she covered her face. The man's hands dropped to his sides and he stood dumb, with starting eyes gazing upon her, trembling and cowering in abject terror.

"She came to me," Girzie went on hoarsely, "proud o' what she had done, and thinking I would be glad tae, when she told me that they were coming to take ye prisoner and that ye would be hanged. I was glad until I minded o' Wattie, and I came to help ye to rin awa' for his sake. O Jeamie Falcon, turn awa' your face if ye ever cared ought for my bairn wha died for ye. Turn awa' your face, that ye mayna be tempted to do your duty, and for his sake let me save his father frae yon cruel death if I can."

Falcon turned his back. Bitterly as he felt toward the Laird, he could not be deaf to the sad appeal of the mother who forgave so much. There was an eloquence in this rough uneducated woman's despair, and her merciful pity for the wretch who had marred her whole life, which awed him into submission. For her sake and for Wattie's, in whose name she pleaded, he was willing yet to give one chance for life to the miserable creature who, now that the blow had fallen, discovered that all his craft had failed him, and remained trembling and speechless, listening intently for any sound of the approaching enemy, and watching Girzie's haggard visage narrowly.

Even in that moment of desperate peril, he suspected the intentions of the only one in the world who was willing to raise a hand on his behalf. Incapable of one generous thought himself, he could not believe that she who had such good reason to detest him could desire to help him. So he stood powerless to move or speak; for the moment she told him of the discovery of the hidden confession, he knew that his cunning had overreached itself at last, and the very means he had taken with the purpose of ridding himself for ever of Carrach, and consequently of all connection with the crime, had turned upon himself. From that day on which greed and selfish fear had induced him to refuse Falcon the farm of Askaig, with what noiseless and sure steps retribution had advanced on him in spite of all his craft, until now, when it culminated in the prison and the gibbet!

"Come awa'," cried Girzie in a feverish whisper the moment she saw Falcon yield to her prayer. "Come awa', if ye want to live. We can get out by the back window and down to the stable maybe afore they come yet. The lads are a' in the kitchen enow at supper, sae naebody will see ye. Come awa'."

Whilst she spoke, she was leading or dragging him to the door of the inner room. The movement seemed to rouse him.

"Stop a minute," he gasped; "I canna gang without siller."

He limped to his desk and tried to unlock it; but his hand trembled so that he could not fit the key in the lock. Girzie, with a sharp cry of impatience, snatched the key from him and opened the desk. He unclosed a secret recess and took out a small leather bag.

" There's no muckle here," he groaned peevishly, " I never kept muckle in the house, and——"

Girzie dragged him away fiercely.

"Come awa', or the only siller ye'll need will be as muckle as buy a shroud."

Shuddering violently at this reminder of his position, he accompanied her with all the speed his terror and infirmity permitted. Girzie closed the door of the inner room and locked it.

Then Falcon drew a long breath of relief, and gazed round the apartment like one awakening from a strange dream. He felt almost stupified by the events which had transpired, and he sat down to recover himself.

But he could not rest. He did not feel satisfied that he had done right in permitting the Laird to escape. He rose and went out to seek Hutcheson. He did not find him at the place where he had told him to wait.

He called, without receiving any answer. He walked slowly in the direction of the steading, peering about him, and calling occasionally. But all he heard was the wind soughing through the trees, and presently the sound of wheels and a horse's feet rattling on the frosty road.

"The fiscal," he muttered, "what am I to say to him?"

He was startled by a shrill shriek breaking suddenly upon the night. He ran in the direction whence the sound proceeded.

Girzie had assisted the Laird through the window of his bedroom, and had followed him herself. As she had stated, the servants were at supper, and they were free from observation. They ran to the stable.

But she did not know that Hutcheson was on the watch. By the light from the kitchen window he had seen them stealing round the house. He was curious to learn the meaning of this stealthy movement, and followed.

Girzie found a lantern in the stable, which

one of the men had left burning to save himself the trouble of relighting it when he returned. She saddled a horse—not the pony, but the strongest and best horse in the stable. The Laird watched her, shivering all the time, but utterly unable to assist her further than to point out the saddle and bridle.

She led the horse out, and was assisting the trembling fugitive to mount, when Hutcheson, suspecting the real meaning of this, darted forward and seized the Laird, dragging him back. The frenzied shriek he uttered the moment Hutcheson touched him was the one which had startled Falcon.

Girzie heard the rattle of the approaching wheels. She was desperate; and she clasped Hutcheson's throat with her long bony fingers, in which was the strength of desperation.

"Let him go," she cried.

She was behind him, the Laird was wrestling in his grasp. He held him with one hand, whilst with the other he endeavoured to unfasten the fingers which were throttling him.

But they held so tightly that he would have been obliged to release the Laird had not the gig they had heard approaching, driven up, stopped beside them, and two men jumped out.

The light from the stable enabled the Laird to recognize the fiscal and Geordie Armstrong, and uttering a stifled cry he fell to the ground writhing in a species of fit.

Girzie instantly released Hutcheson; he turned, and would have seized her, but Falcon, who had reached the spot almost instantaneously with the fiscal, stayed him.

She shrunk away, seeing that it was all over, that her help had come too late.

CHAPTER XII.

PROOFS.

"O, front of brass and brain of ass,
  With heart of hare compounded;
How are thy boasts repaid with costs,
  And all thy pride confounded!"—*Old Ballad.*

The paper which Mrs. Begg had seen the
Laird hiding under the large stone that lay
loose in front of the Clashgirn door, and
which she had carried to the fiscal, revealed
the manner in which Wattie Todd met his
death. It purported to be written to Carrach's dictation by his mate Donald on board
the schooner *Ailsa*, and showed that both
Carrach and the Laird were mistaken as to
the identity of the man who had fallen.

Donald, being questioned, denied all knowledge of the paper, and wrote a few words of
it under the fiscal's direction, displaying quite
a different style of caligraphy. Mr. Carnegie

thereupon closely examined the penmanship, and, in spite of the careful attempt at disguise, proved it to be McWhapple's own by comparison with letters in his possession which were undoubtedly written by him.

After explaining that the confession was made to ease his conscience, and to show that he was not so guilty as might be supposed, the statement proceeded—and it is only necessary to give here the portions which explain the little that was left dark after Donald's confession and the Laird's revelation to Falcon:—

"I hung about Askaig all day in order to make sure that James Falcon quitted the place that night. I had been drinking whisky during the night before and during the day; and I had two bottles with me when Donald went away. My head was not clear, for besides drinking much, I had not had any sleep. As the storm grew louder I stole up to the barn which faces the door of Askaig house and hid myself there. It was dark then, and I had no fear of being seen.

"I saw Cairnieford arrive, and heard his horse clattering away soon afterwards. I looked out again and then crept over to the window. Cairnieford and his mistress were still there. So was Falcon. They were quarrelling. I was nearly caught by Rab Keith, but he went into the house without seeing me. I was going to creep back to the barn when Cairnieford ran out. He sought round the place, I supposed for his horse. He nearly came upon me two or three times, but it was so dark that he had no chance of seeing me except when the lightning flashed. He was muttering in a daft way to himself. I saw him pass the door again, and that was the last I saw of him.

"Rab Keith came out, shouting something that I could not hear for the noise of the spate and the wind and the rain. He came close to me, and I crept round to the back of the house to get out of his way. I do not know how long I stopped there, maybe half an hour; then I started to get to the window again or the barn—I cannot mind which of them I was going to—·but when I turned the corner of the house next the road I knocked against a man, who clutched at me and caught the end of a plaid I was wearing. He shouted something, but I broke from him and ran. I'm a heavy man, and not a quick runner. The chiel' kept at my heels, and I found myself at the fence of the Brownie's Bite.

The chiel' griped me again, and a flash of lightning let me see that it was Falcon who had hold of me; and I supposed that he knew me at the same time, for he grasped me tighter. I strove with him, trying to break away from him, but he held on. I tried to throw him down, but he got the plaid with his teeth and his hands clasped round my neck. I got savage at that, struck him, and flung him from me. I heard the fence crack, loud as the wind blew—I heard an awful skirl, loud as the spate roared—and I knew that Falcon had gone over the Bite. I ran away from the place, and will never go near it again if I can help it.

"I did not like the chiel' because he was

trying to harm me. But when I struck him I had no thought of anything more than just to gar him let go; when I flung him from me I had forgot that we were on the brow of the Bite. I was not meaning to kill him; it was an accident; and it might have happened to me as well as to him. I was sorry for him; but I could not expect other folk to believe that it was an accident; and so I mean to keep clear of the place. All this is solemn truth."

his

IVAN × CARRACH.

mark

Witness—JEANIE GRAY.

This paper Jeanie identified without hesitation as the one she had signed; and the spots of ink made by the pen slipping when Carrach had been drawing his mark were there. Her signature to the receipt which had been placed in the fiscal's hands so freely was declared to be a forgery. That explained why the Laird had refused to show the document to Mr. Carnegie and Jeanie. He required time to trace her name on a docu-

ment which would be harmless to himself
and comparatively so to Carrach.

That same night the fiscal removed his
three prisoners to the safe keeping of the
county jail. The Laird was in such a condition that he required constant attendance,
and the doctor said he doubted if he would
ever recover from the shock.

Of course there was a fine ado in the Port
when scraps of the singular story got about,
dressed up with all the fantastic ornaments
in which gossip delights to array her subjects.
The kirk folk lingered much longer than
usual amongst the tombstones next day, and
there was a very general opinion that Jeanie
was a fine body, James Falcon was an honest
lad, and that Robin Gray had been hasty.
There were very few who really understood
the generous natures of all three, which had
been so severely tried by the petty machina-
tions of a man whose guilty conscience sought
protection from unknown dangers.

Geordie Armstrong was a man of high
importance on this day. His diligence had

been commended by the fiscal; and everybody
was anxious to speak to him, as he was supposed to know all the ins and outs of the
strange story.   So Geordie, who had always
been sensible of his own consequence, fancied
that the folk were at last beginning to recognize his merit.   They had laughed at him
for the many blunders he had committed in
his official capacity when, as he thought—
with some reason possibly—that most of
them would have made the same blunder
under the same circumstances.

For instance, when Adam Lindsay's cow
had been "lifted," Geordie had set off in hot
pursuit of the thief to Glasgow in consequence
of having been told that a man had been seen
driving a cow in that direction.   He had not
paused to learn what the beast or the man
was like, and on his way to the city he had
overtaken several cows and several men.
Having thus a selection of possible criminals
he made his choice accordingly.   But, to the
utter confusion of his charge, the cow proved
to be a fine stirk; and soon afterwards good

reasons were found for believing that Lindsay's beast had been driven off to Sanquhar, the direction upon which Geordie had obstinately turned his back.

He was much laughed at for this and similar misadventures; but he had at length obtained an opportunity to distinguish himself, and he made the most of it.

He was up early on this Sabbath morning, and before kirk-time he took a stroll down by the Links. He passed the place where Jeanie had been seized by Carrach, but of course the mounds displayed no traces of a struggle, and the tide had washed out all imprints on the beach. Geordie had taken his notion of seeking corroboration of Mrs. Gray's statement of her forcible abduction from the fact that the fiscal had made much of the footprints on the brow of the Brownie's Bite, and he began to think that he was to be disappointed.

With his disappointment he began to scent a new mystery. What if he should be able to present quite a new version of the affair

—or, at any rate, that part of it which related to Mrs. Gray's voyage? Vanity assumes the most dangerous shape when it tempts a man to an effort to prove his own exceeding cleverness. Geordie was exactly in that state of mind now.

He looked about with profound suspicion of something not perfectly correct in Mrs. Gray's deposition. Luckily for himself, and perhaps for others, whilst he looked and meditated he discovered the small anchor by which Carrach had secured the boat when he landed. The Laird having cut the rope to bind Jeanie, the anchor had been forgotten in the Highlander's hurry to get away with his double prize. Geordie was unable to associate the anchor with the affair, but he took it in charge on suspicion, as he would have done the beach itself if he had only been able to carry it on his shoulder. March-ing off with his discovery and crossing the Links he next found Jeanie's plaid.

That changed the whole current of his thoughts. For although he did not recognize the plaid as Mrs. Gray's, not being afflicted with too many ideas at a time—which might have led to the suggestion that the plaid belonged to somebody else—he at once concluded that it was hers, and became as pompously proud to be able to present corroboration of her testimony as he might have been to throw doubt on it.

He made the most of his discovery to the few farmers and townsfolk whom he was disposed to admit to any degree of confidence on this important occasion. It really proved of some little advantage in the long chain of evidence which had been welded together through so many remarkable events.

There seemed to be no chink by which the culprits might hope to escape; and much as the Laird had been looked up to in the town as a man of means and an elder, there was little sympathy expressed for his miserable position, even amongst those douce bodies with whom he had most associated. It was hard, perhaps, but it was none the less just; all the years he had spent in greedy striving

after respect had only obtained for him the
outward show of it, and that not from many.
There was no heart in it; there had been
none in his own hard dry nature to influence
that of others by the magical attraction of
sincerity.   He had offered to his little world
a mockery of piety and truth, and he obtained
in return a mockery of respect.

Those who had disliked him and openly
shown it in the day of his prosperity were
mercifully silent now.   But those who had
disliked him and restrained their tongues,
either in consequence of his position or in
doubt of their own convictions, spoke now in
many voices.   Those who had bartered with
him, and consulted with him on affairs of
kirk or burgh, marvelled that they had been
so long deceived by him.   None pitied him.

But everybody pitied Girzie Todd.   All
day there were little groups of fishers, townsfolk and country folk, at the cross, about the
market-place, at door-steps, and down at the
Port, in grave consultation about the whole
business.   A few kindly neighbours sought

Girzie with the hope of "cheering her a wee;" but her cot was empty; and Dawnie, the cuddie, was ungratefully taking advantage of the occasion, to make a raid through the patch of garden, and feast on the green "curlies." He was driven into his shed, and made fast. One sensible dame, who had been the first to enter Girzie's house, finding the little heap of money on the table, had, after a moment's wonder at the wealth which was thus carelessly exposed to the first rogue who might happen to enter, gathered it up, replaced it in the old stocking which was lying beside it, and hid the precious parcel under the bed, to be ready for the rightful owner when she might return.

There was no doubt entertained as to the cause of Girzie's absence. She had gone to Clashgirn to watch by dead Wattie's side, until the morning came, when he was to be buried.

As soon as she had seen her attempt to enable McWhapple to escape frustrated, she had turned away with the bitter resignation

of one who feels that a judgment has fallen,
and who is conscious that all effort to with-
stand it is futile. It did not surprise her;
she had expected it from the moment she had
learned the truth from Mrs. Begg; and
although she had tried to save the man, she
had done so with little hope of success. Now
she was satisfied; there was nothing left for
her to do but submit to the fate in which
she recognized the retribution of the past.

She had crept up to the dark room where
the body was lying, and crouched down
beside it. She uttered no moan, no despairing wail now. In a sort of stupor she remained; and to everybody who ventured to
look in on her with kindly intent to offer her
food or comfort, she would not answer otherwise than by a dull absent stare, which
frightened the simple folks. Even Falcon
could not obtain more from her than a piteous request that he would leave her alone
with her bairn. He obeyed her; for he saw
that the attempt to console only irritated her.

He was himself in a state of irritation,

which all the efforts of Hutcheson failed to
soothe. In a rough hearty way the sailor
endeavoured to present a cheery view of the
future to his comrade; for his own part he
could not understand how a man coming into
a considerable fortune, as Falcon was, could
hang his head and look discontented.

"Man, what's the use o' fortune," exclaimed
the master of Clashgirn, "when one has lost
the power to enjoy it? What's the use o' a
horse to a man that can neither ride nor
drive?"

"He can learn to do baith," answered
Hutcheson readily.

Falcon turned away from him abruptly: it
was impossible to make him see or feel as he
did. But he was sensible that his conduct
must appear contradictory to other persons,
and he did not blame Hutcheson for being
puzzled by it. He had striven so hard to
achieve a certain end, and now that it seemed
so near realization, he was behaving as if he
would have liked to undo all that he had
done. That did seem ridiculous.

But he had no desire to undo it; nay, he said to himself that, if the circumstances were to be repeated, he could not act otherwise than he had done. It was only the reaction of the excitement he had been undergoing which made him restless and gloomy. Whilst there had been work for him to do, whilst Robin Gray's fate was uncertain, and Jeanie's pale anxious face was spurring him to exertion, he had not had time to think much of the future. But the work accomplished, the strain relaxed, and he saw that with his own hand he had helped to raise the mountain which separated him for ever from the one creature in the world who could have given his life purpose and joy. He would not have been human if some of the old bitterness had not returned to disturb his peace. He wished with all his soul that there had never been such a person as Robin Gray in the world, although he could not wish that he had refused his help in saving him from an unmerited doom.

"Look here, mate," said Hutcheson—they

were down by the shore, the only place where Falcon felt at all at ease; "I ken what's wrang wi' ye. You're in a way about your auld lass. Weel, wha kens whether she mayna be a widow ere lang."

Falcon started and looked angry at this utterance of a thought which had once occurred to himself, and which he had manfully cast from him.

"I'm owing you one or two good turns, Hutcheson," he said, griping him by the arm and shaking him to make his words more emphatic; "but if ye say that again we'll hae a quarrel."

"As broken ships hae come to land," muttered Hutcheson, but he discreetly kept the opinion to himself.

"I would be shamed for mysel' if I could find ony pleasure in waiting for a dead man's shoon," Falcon went on proudly, but with more of sorrow than anger in his tone now. "No, Hutcheson, if ever I'm to ken what pleasure is again it'll be out yonder on the sea amidst storm and battle."

."Do ye mean to say ye're gaun to sea again now that ye hae got a fortune and can do as ye like?"

"I'm going as soon as ever my affairs are settled, and Mistress Gray's guidman is safe delivered from jail."

Hutcheson began to whistle, remembered that it was Sabbath, and checked himself, but said nothing. He liked Falcon more and more every day, and he had his own opinion about the whole business, which was that it might have been better for all parties if it had been Cairnieford who had tumbled over the Brownie's Bite instead of daft Wattie Todd. He had a presentiment that something might happen yet to alter the present aspect of affairs, and so he held his tongue and waited.

CHAPTER XIII.

IN PRISON.

" Brightest climes shall mirk appear,
    Desert ilka blooming shore;
  Till the fates, nae mair severe,
    Friendship, love, and peace restore."—*Anon.*

The sudden revulsion from doubt to confidence which had taken place in Robin Gray's breast at the revelation of Jeanie's faith in him, left him in utter shame of the cruel ignominy he had cast on her; in utter shame of the passion which had betrayed him, and transformed a man of some common sense into a mad blind fool. He had smarted sharply for it all after she had left him, and there was scarcely an epithet of contempt which he had not applied to himself.

But the revulsion had given him hope, too. He had, previous to her visit, been indifferent as to how the charge might stand against him; he did not mean to make the least effort to save himself, and had not Mr. Carnegie taken up the case promptly on his own authority, the person most concerned would not have instructed him to do it.

But now he was like a man who had been shut up in a dark cell, and who is suddenly lifted out to the broad glare of the sun. The light dazzled him at first, and he scarcely knew what he was to do. She had said, "Dinna be dooncast," and "Take courage!" and the words and the voice remained with him, cheering and comforting him.

He did take courage, and the first act of his new spirit was to get the fiscal to send for Jeanie that he might have her forgiveness before he made any effort to save his life. Until he knew that she would forgive him, he did not care to live; if she refused, it would be easier for him to accept the fate which threatened him than to endure perhaps years of torture.

The fiscal good-naturedly sent a messenger to the lawyer's office to inquire for Mrs.

Gray; but she had gone from there, and Mr. Carnegie begged that she might not be interfered with at present.

Cairnieford had waited impatiently for the return of the messenger, and he would have had him start again in search of Jeanie; but the fiscal advised him to be calm, and wait, especially as there was no time then to seek her. He yielded, because he could not help himself, and that afternoon he was conveyed to the county prison to await the issue of events.

He had little fear that the result would prove his innocence, however strong the proof might appear against him then. It was not the verdict of judge and jury he dreaded. It was Jeanie's verdict which concerned him most. If she could only see him then; if she could only hear him whilst the shadow of the scaffold was still lowering on him, she might be able to feel how bitterly he repented the folly and the wrong which in his frenzy he had perpetrated.

The night passed, and she did not come.

He moved about restlessly in his narrow cell during the dark hours. He could not sleep, and the events of the week flitted across his brain with the vividness of reality. The Laird was at the bottom of it all; it was his infernal sneers which had first roused him, which had first started his suspicions, and his own fury had done the rest. He cursed the pitiful wretch with all the fierceness of which his nature was capable.

When dawn came, and a pale streak of light penetrated the cell, he was exhausted by the night of torture he had spent, and he stretched himself on the rough bed of straw; but not to sleep. He lay listening to every step that crossed the stone corridors, sickening with disappointment when it stopped short of his door or passed by it.

The day passed like the night, and still there had come no message. He was wrought up to a pitch of nervous excitement which threatened a violent fever, when at a late hour the fiscal himself entered the cell with a lantern in his hand, and a grin on his face.

He took a good survey of the prisoner before he spoke.

Robin stared at him with the blank expression of one in doubt whether the person he sees is friend or foe; and then, eagerly approaching him, he cried—

"Is onything wrang, sir? Hae ye ony news for me? Is my wife weel, or——"

"Quietly, quietly, Cairnieford," interrupted the fiscal in his cheeriest tone; "one question at a time, if ye please, and before I say a word, understand this: I am here as your friend, not the fiscal. You see as your friend I may speak to you in a way that would scarcely do if I were here in my official capacity."

"I understand, sir, and thank ye. It's kind o' ye, I'm sure; and ye may count on me laying nae stress on what ye may say if ye should need to alter your words hereafter."

He was choking with anxiety to hear something about Jeanie; he did not think of asking anything about his own fate.

"That's right," said Mr. Smart; "and
I'm glad to say that I hae good news for
ye."

"She's weel, then—she'll come to see me
again?"

"Your guidwife?—Oh, aye, she was brawly
when I saw her last about three hours syne;
and I hope ye'll be able to save her the
trouble o' coming to see ye here by going to
see her yoursel'."

" Eh—What ?"

"Now, mind, it's Matthew Smart, no the
fiscal, that's speaking."

"Aye, aye, I mind."

"Weel, then, there's been a mistake some
way. The fiscal was misled by the information he got; but he's no a fool, and he's no
afraid to own a mistake, especially when the
circumstances were of such a kind as to mis-
lead anybody. So the chances are that, as
soon as the needful formalities hae been gone
through, you'll be set free. That will be
maybe on Monday forenoon."

" Free!" echoed Cairnieford, puzzled to

know by what magic his position had been so happily changed.

"Aye, free, that's the word, and as clear o' ony suspicion o' guilt as if ye had never been here. I told you at the time I would rather that anybody had had the job but me, and I come here now to show ye that I spoke honestly by giving ye the earliest news o' your good luck."

"But how—how has it come about? I'm dazed a wee by it a'—it's sae sudden."

"You hae your guidwife—I wish half the women folk had half her sense and courage —you hae her to thank and James Falcon."

"Falcon!" roared Cairnieford, starting bewildered, and frowning.

"Aye, just him; it wasna him, but Girzie Todd's lad, Wattie, wha was killed. That was what misled me—I mean the fiscal."

And then he explained all that had occurred as it had been laid before him, always reminding his interlocutor that he spoke purely in his private character as a friend, and that something might happen before

Monday to cause him to speak quite differently as an officer of justice. He had no fear of that, however, and being a kindly-hearted man he was really glad of the opportunity to redeem, in some measure, the inconvenience —to say nothing of the peril—which Cairnieford had suffered from the singular combination of circumstances which had led to his incarceration.

When he had finished he was surprised to find Robin silent and even gloomy.

"Why, man, what's wrang wi' ye?" exclaimed Mr. Smart. "I thought ye would hae been louping for joy; instead o' that ye look as though I had brought word that your execution would take place on Monday."

"Falcon no dead," he muttered abstractedly, his hands wandering nervously over his head, whilst he stared hard at the floor.

"No!—are ye sorry for that?"

Robin was roused by the sharp question.

"Sorry?—the Lord forbid. It's a shame o' me to look ungrateful; but, man, if ye had tholed what I hae tholed on his account ye wouldna find it an easy matter to accept sae muckle favour at his hands. Lord forgie me, but I feel amaist as though I would rather hae been left here to dee than owe my life to ought that he has done. Maybe it's because I hae done him sic sair wrang that his kindness dunts sae hard on me."

"Hoots, man, that's no like the honest chiel' I took ye for. But ye'll think better o't before Monday; and I hope then ye'll gie the lad your hand, and say you're sorry for your mistake, as I hae done wi' you."

The fiscal retired, and Robin, in the dark again, sat down on his stool, covering his face with his hands. He winced cruelly as he thought how much more noble James Falcon must appear in her eyes than he could ever hope to do.

" But he wasna tempted as I hae been," he muttered bitterly; "he wasna deceived as I hae been, or he couldna hae shown himsel' ony better nor me."

How his name was coupled with hers— how, in everything she had done, Falcon had been there to help her! It was not easy to bear the thought of all that.

But a happier spirit obtained sway in his heart, with the memory that all Jeanie had done, and all she had suffered, had been for his sake. His breast heaved, a big sob escaped him, and the strong man wept sad tears of repentance alone in the darkness of his prison. They brought him relief: they seemed to bring him light; and in the morning he was calm, grateful for the service which had been rendered him, and prepared to make honest acknowledgment of it.

CHAPTER XIV.

BY THE GRAVE.

"Nae wrang can rouse, nae slight can move
The dead frae sleep that quenches pain;
Nae magic in the voice o' love
Can make the cauld heart beat again."—*Anon.*

On the Monday forenoon Mr. Carnegie arrived at the jail accompanied by Mr. Monduff. The necessary arrangements for liberating Robin had been made with a rapidity unexampled in the history of legal proceedings. The truth was, that the fiscal had exerted himself to dispose of the matter with the least possible delay, and now the worthy lawyer in a fussy way, and the minister in his quiet hearty fashion, congratulated their friend on his release.

The doors were open for him to go, the dog-cart was waiting outside to convey him to Portlappoch, and, to the surprise of both gentlemen, he did not show any hurry to quit his prison.

He received their congratulations with a serious face, looking all the while over their shoulders, as if expecting to see somebody else. After he had thanked them in a quiet tone—not the tone of a man who has just been rescued from the gallows—he said—

"She hasna come wi' ye?"

They understood then what was the matter, and the lawyer looked uncomfortable, blurting out with some hesitation and awkwardness—

"No, ye see she's had a great deal to do, and she has overworked herself: and, besides, ye cannot expect——"

He was checked by a motion of Mr. Monduff's hand. The minister took Robin's arm in a kindly grasp.

"You'll no be long until you see her, have no fear of that, Cairnieford. The woman who could do what she has done for you must have that in her heart which will make her glad to welcome you when she learns that you place any value on her welcome."

"Value on her welcome! Oh, man, I care nought for a' the world's welcome if she be na ane to say it's weel I hae been spared—it's weel nae shame is on me"—(huskily and unsteadily, in spite of every effort to conceal the weakness).

"Aye, but she does not know that. Remember how you parted with her, and then set yourself with all your might to prove to her that, whatever you may have thought, felt, or said in passion, you see how false it all was, now that you are calm."

"Thank ye, sir, for that; it gie's me courage and hope too. I will prove to her that I ken her worth, and how cruelly I hae tried it."

"Adam has gone back to his old home," broke in the lawyer, "and Mrs. Gray went there this morning."

After that Robin was eager to get back to the Port. They started in the dog-cart with a parting salute from the fiscal, who happened to appear in the court at the

moment. On the way, Mr. Carnegie gave
Robin a fuller account of all that had transpired than the fiscal had been able to do;
and explained to him how Falcon turned
out to be the son of Hugh Sutherland and
the master of Clashgirn.

"I suspected that lang syne," Cairnieford
observed drily, "and I told ye o't at the time
they were burying the lady, but ye wouldna
hear o' sic a thing."

"What could I do on a mere suspicion
without a grain o' proof o' ony sort to back
it? Besides, I must confess that I was deceived by the man's pawky way—very much
deceived."

Mr. Monduff interrupted the conversation
by asking Cairnieford if he would attend the
funeral of Wattie Todd.

"I think it is a duty you owe the poor lad
and yourself," he said, "for nothing will
better satisfy the folk of your sorrow for his
misfortune."

"Poor Wattie! I will go, not because it
matters to me, but because I liked him."

They were driving along the highroad, and would enter the town at the head of the main street, where the kirk stood. The steeple was in sight when Mr. Monduff spoke, and as they approached they perceived that the gate of the churchyard was open. They dismounted at the manse.

Looking down the street, Robin saw a long procession slowly advancing up the brae. He stood by the gate with Mr. Carnegie. First came the coffin borne by four men, the two at the head wearing the garb of sailors, the other two the ordinary dress of the fishermen of the Port. Following behind the coffin came Girzie, a large 'kerchief thrown over her head concealing her features, and held tight under her chin by her hand. She walked with head bent, apparently unconscious of everything around her. Occasionally her eyes were raised from the ground, but only to rest a moment on the coffin, and then with a dull weary expression to droop slowly to the ground again. A long band of fishers and country folk followed in their everyday attire, having apparently just quitted their work to join the procession as it passed along; and, by this simple act of respect, expressing their sympathy with the mother. Hard weather-beaten faces most of them, dull and common-place features, but with a sober shade upon them now, that betokened the sincerity of the feeling which had prompted them to follow poor Wattie to his grave. The rough gar-ments, the unkempt hair and unwashed faces, all suggestive of busy struggling life, and the devout silence in which they listened to the minister's prayer, imparted by contrast a solemnity to the proceedings that no finery of mourning attire could have heightened.

Robin, with head uncovered like the rest, stood beside the new-made grave. His gaze was fixed upon the ground, and he did not notice the man who stood opposite him on the other side of the pit. The man was one of those who had been bearing the bier, and as soon as he had laid it down, took his place with head bowed, whilst the minister pro-ceeded with his sad duty.

Girzie stood at the foot of the grave motionless. Her hands tightened their grip on the 'kerchief under her chin, and she frowned, as if the effort to restrain her emotion from the wild outburst for which it was struggling, gave her cause for anger with every one around her. When the first shovelful of earth rattled on the coffin, she started and glanced quickly down into the pit as if about to throw herself into it. Then, with a glance about her, but uttering no sound of grief, she sat down on a neighbouring tombstone, covering her face as if she shrunk from the compassionating gaze of her friends.

The crowd slowly dispersed as the work of filling up the grave went on. The folk returned to their avocations to laugh, to joke, to sigh and struggle, and to remember this day with shaking of the head whenever they saw the silent woman pass amongst them.

Robin looked up, and recognized in the man opposite him James Falcon. The latter drew back, as if he would avoid an encounter

between them. Robin hesitated: he winced
at the duty he saw before him, but he was no
coward, and he would not shirk anything he
felt he ought to do. He stretched out his
hand to Falcon, beckoning him back. The
latter halted, looked doubtfully at Cairnieford,
and at the grave. Then he made a step
nearer, as if drawn by some influence from
the dead.

"James Falcon, or Mister Sutherland, as I
understand ye should be called now, will ye
speak wi' me a minute? It's easier to be for-
giving in the presence o' death than when
we're in the pride o' health and strength. I
doubt it's my fault, and maybe partly yours,
that Wattie Todd's lying in the moulds enow;
and ye canna refuse to hear me afore the sod
is laid ower him."

"I'm listening"—(somewhat shyly).

"I want to speir a question first. You
ken what it is to care mair for ae body than
for a' the world, and a' that's in't beside. Tell
me then, if you had been in my place at
Askaig, what would ye hae done?"

Falcon was silent, gazing darkly at the ground.

"If every thought ye had," Robin went on in a low agitated voice, "had been linked to her; if every hope had sprung frae her, if she had been light and joy and hame to ye, if she had been a' that heart could care for or head could think about, and ye had been cheated wi' suspicions o' her, poisoned wi' doubts o' her by a leeing tongue and by strange circumstances—tell me, sir, what ye would hae done in my place?"

With an impulsive jerk of his body, Falcon answered—"I would have been blind and mad as you were, I believe."

"It was an honest man that answered me. Will you take my hand now, for I feel nae shame in asking ye to pardon whatever wrang I hae done ye——"

"Whisht, Cairnieford," cried Falcon, interrupting him and wringing his hand warmly, "forget that if ye can; let it be buried there in poor Wattie's grave; and some day—years after this, long weary years they maun be to me, but happy ones to you, I hope—maybe you and your wife will be able to call me a friend."

"I call ye that now, and I am grateful to ye for letting me do it. I can feel something o' what ye hae sacrificed in helping me. But, sir, when I thought you were in trouble, I sought you to offer ye help, and to bid ye welcome to my house. Ye ken how I was cheated, and I only ask ye to judge me by what ye might hae thought and done yoursel' under the same circumstances."

"I do that. . . . I am glad you have called me a friend, and I'll try to prove mysel' worthy o' the name by quitting the Port as soon as I can. She says it is better so, and she is right—God bless her."

He spoke these latter words very huskily. They shook hands again; and Robin went away to seek his wife, feeling more satisfied with himself and everybody else now that he had made peace with Falcon than he had done for many days.

Mr. Carnegie had informed him that Adam,

unshaken by the passing events or the per-
suasions of the doctor, had on Saturday removed with Mrs. Lindsay to their own home.
Jeanie had gone to Cairnieford on the Saturday night after the Laird's arrest, to place
things in readiness for the anticipated return
of the master.

With a full heart she had arranged the
household just in the manner in which he
most liked to see it. His chair was placed at
the proper angle to the fire; his whips were
hung up behind the door; his thick staff, which
he used when going across the fields to look
at the sheep or the cattle, was in the corner
where he always sought it first, although he
never placed it there himself; his bonnet and
his plaid were laid on the little side-table
near the window, as she had been accustomed
to place them on the nights preceding mar-
ket-days.

Then after she had arranged everything
ready to his hand, she had sat down on his
chair and stared blankly round the place,
saying to herself in a dull stupified sort of

way, whilst something was throbbing and
swelling in her breast—

"It's the last time I'll sort them for ye,
Robin, the last time I'll sit here in the hame
that was growing sae bright. Aye, but it's
grown dark—dark noo, and I canna see the
light o't onymair. . . . Lord, watch ower't
and leave some glint o' pleasure in it for him.
I never ken'd a' thae things sae weel as I do
the-day. I never thought I could hae found
it sae hard to part wi' them."

And then the strength, which the excitement of all she had had to do gave her, broke
down, and she cried in a sad quiet way. She
could scarcely manage to walk to her father's
cottage on Monday morning. She succeeded
by a great effort, and there Mr. Monduff and
Mr. Carnegie had found her when they had
wanted to persuade her to go with them for
Robin, and there Robin sought her now.

The cottage had already resumed something of its old appearance. A net was hanging on the wall, oars were resting against
the simple porch, and smoke was rising from

the chimney. In the old days Robin had been accustomed to lift the latch and walk in; but now he knocked.

Adam himself answered the summons, and became unusually stiff and stern the moment he recognized the visitor.

" I'm glad to see ye on the right side o' the jail, sir," was his grim salutation.

"Thank ye, Adam, though ye look as if ye were rather angry than glad at sight o' me. Weel, ye had reason to be angry wi' me; but I own I was in the wrang, and I hae suffered for't. Dinna bear ill-will against me longer than you can help."

" I bear nae ill-will"—(stiff as ever).

" Is Jeanie here?"

" My dochter is here, and let me tell ye at once that ye canna see her enow, if that's what ye came here for. She's put a' things right for ye at your ain house, and now she's clean wrought out. She's ta'en her bed ——"

" Is she no weel?"

" She's no weel ava, and the doctor says she's no to be fashed, and she said hersel' that if ye should come seeking her, I was to tell ye she couldna see ye, and she sha'na."

"May I no speak ae word to her? just to beg her no to think waur o' me than I deserve."

"She doesna need ye to tell her that. Man, she thocht ower kindly o' ye even when ye were scorning her."

Robin turned his face from the stern old man, who was as hard and immovable as flint.

"Tell her," he said in a broken voice, "that I'll come here every day until she lets me speak to her—until she lets me hear frae her ain lips that she canna and winna forgive me."

He did not stay to say more or hear Adam's answer.

He went to the doctor, and from him learned that Jeanie was in a state of low fever, brought on by excessive exertion of body and anxiety of mind. The excitement had sustained her whilst there was work to do; but the work completed, her husband safe, the collapse followed.

"What she has gone through," said the doctor finally, "would have killed many a woman in her condition, and I advise you to be careful to do nothing that may agitate her."

Robin went away. He knew now that unexplained other reason for her truth to him at which she had hinted. He was welcomed home by the farm folk with hearty rejoicing; but the home was bleak and cheerless without her. He could not rest, he could not live in it without her, and he rose with a passionate moan to quit the place.

Then he checked himself; became calmer, and with bowed head and sad face set himself to work and wait, hoping. Day after day he was at the cottage, always to receive the same dry answer from Adam—

"My dochter's doing brawly, but she's no fit to see onybody."

Robin, bearing in mind the doctor's warning, would not press his request yet a while. He watched and waited.

CHAPTER XV.

SETTLING DAY.

"The seas may row, the winds may blow,
    And swathe me round wi' danger;
My native land I must forego,
    And roam a lonely stranger."—*From the Gaelic.*

Carrach's conduct did not alter in the jail,
except so far as the shade of difference which
might be distinguished between sullen silence
and dull indifference. The fiscal tried every
means in his power to obtain a statement
from him of some sort. But the Highlander
doggedly refused to say anything even in his
own defence.

At length the fiscal, hoping to rouse him,
told him that there was important evidence
against him.

"Was there?" said Carrach, rolling his eyes
in the slow ox-like manner peculiar to him;

"oich, but she was sorry for that, and wha was the evidence?"

"Donald, your mate, and the Laird."

"Did they'll told ye all about it?"

"Yes."

"Then what'll you want me to told you again for?"

"For your own sake and to get at the truth as nearly as possible."

At that Carrach gave a species of grunt which might have been intended for a laugh or an oath, but which certainly intimated that he did not take much interest in the pursuit of truth. He picked up a straw from the heap which formed his couch, put it in his mouth and began deliberately to chew it. After a pause—

"Where was the Laird?" he inquired.

"Not far away."

"Where was that?"

"In the second cell from this; a prisoner like yourself"—(surely that will make him speak out, the fiscal thought).

But the skipper coolly chewed the straw

and rolled his eyes without displaying the least concern in tone or manner, whilst he said—

"In shail—ochone, but that was a fall doon. Well, you'll shust go to him. He'll told you what you'll want to know. I'll no spoke a word—Pe-tam."

He adhered to that resolution, and with stolid placidity awaited the turn of events.

The Laird's conduct was that of abject terror. His limbs seemed to be paralyzed, so that when he was laid on the straw heap which served as bed in the cell, he lay there for several days apparently incapable of rising.

He started wildly whenever any of the warders entered the cell, and shook as with the ague so long as he remained near him. He whined piteously at times, lamenting in a childish, helpless manner the misfortune that had befallen him. At other times he would shriek out with hysterical vehemence that he was innocent, and that he would have everybody hanged or transported at least for the slander which had brought him to this pass.

On several occasions during the night he had started apparently from sleep uttering wild shrieks of terror which echoed along the stone corridors of the prison, until one of the turnkeys entered his cell with a light. Then his cries subsided into a piteous whine, and he implored the man to leave the light with him—the darkness was so horrible. It was clear that his reason had been affected by the discovery of his knavery and the dread of its consequences.

His frenzy reached a climax when he was visited by the sheriff-depute and the fiscal for the purpose of taking his deposition.

Mr. Smart entered first, and at sight of him the Laird started to a sitting posture, drawing his knees up to his chin almost, and clutching the straw under him with the spasmodic grip of a drowning man, whilst his body quivered and writhed as with intense physical pain. His pale ferrety eyes blinked, and his lips moved as if he were trying to speak; but he had no command over his tongue.

His terror was pitiable. The fiscal stepped over to him and held an open snuff-box towards him. The blinking eyes darted from the fiscal's face to the box, and back; a hideous girn twisted his features, and he uttered a shrill sort of laugh that grated like a harsh false note on the ear. His hand, shaking violently, dipped into the box, and as he filled his nostrils with the tobacco he obtained speech—

"Od, it's extraordinar'!"—(a high sharp tone and the girn still twisting his features) —"ye come an' offer me the prime consolation o' my miserable existence, and me thought ye was coming to take me awa' to the wuddie —no, I dinna mean that"—(checking himself with fierce shrillness)—"ye couldna do that —ye haena the power to do it. I'm wrangfully accused. I'm a martyred man, but I'll hae the law, sir. I'll hae ye put through your facings to a tune ye dinna bargain for. I'll hae——wha's you?"

His fit of passion disappeared as his eyes blinked at the sheriff, and all his shivering fear returned.

" Take another pinch, Laird," said the fiscal quietly; " it'll do ye guid."

" Wha's yon?"—(taking a pinch, or rather a handful, half of which was scattered over his breast on the way to his nostrils).

" A friend, come to hear what information you can give us about this extraordinary business."

" I hae nae information to give, sir, I ken naething about it——"

The fiscal interrupted this new burst of vehemence.

" I should tell you, Laird, that the only chance I see for yoursel' is in making a clean breast of it and telling us everything."

The wretched prisoner's eyes blinked suspiciously from one to the other of his visitors as if he were eager to discover how far he might trust them, and how he might speak most to his own advantage. Weak and helpless as he was, he clung to life with the des-

perate tenacity of one whose doom meets him
face to face.

"There is no other chance for you, Laird,"
added the fiscal quietly.

He snatched at the chance with feverish
anxiety.

"Do you think that?—do you really think
that?"

"I'm sure of it."

"And—and if I tell ye—that is, if I had
onything to tell ye and would tell ye—will
it gie me a chance to win out o' this?"

"Surely, surely."

The prospect sufficed; he was ready to confess anything that might help to save himself; he did not care who suffered so long as
he might escape.

He bore testimony to the fidelity of what
he had written as Carrach's confession. Except in regard to the opening statement as to
the circumstances under which it had been
written, it was correct in every particular.
The events it recorded had been impressed
on his mind with a too painful distinctness

by his own dread of being implicated in the crime for him to have made an error in any item. He supplied the necessary links to establish the identity of James Falcon as the son of the late Hugh Sutherland, and removed every obstacle to his taking possession of the estate.

When he had finished he seemed to be exhausted by his exertions, but he pleaded piteously for mercy.

"They winna hang me, fiscal," he cried, "it wasna me that did it. I'm an innocent man; they wouldna hang a poor creature like me."

"You are not like to die on the gallows," said the fiscal, to soothe him as he retired with the sheriff.

The Laird shrieked with ecstasy; then suddenly became silent and cunningly observant of all that passed around him, as if already calculating how he might turn it to future account.

He was quieter that afternoon than he had been since he had been imprisoned. He was

quieter, too, during the night than he had
been previously. The warders heard him
groan two or three times; but they heard
none of the wild frenzied shrieks with which
he had formerly roused the echoes of the
silent prison. The change was remarkable
as well as a relief.

Early in the morning, when the warder
entered his cell, he found the Laird quiet
enough—he was dead. His body was twisted
as if he had died in acute pain, and his eyes
glared wider than they had ever done in life.
He looked as if death had taken him by surprise. It was the miserable end of a miserable career.

Carrach was tried at the next circuit
court. There were two charges against him;
first, the murder of Wattie Todd; and second,
the wilful burning of the brig called the
Colin, to the danger of human life and the
defrauding of the underwriters. In this latter
case—the second in the indictment, although
the first in occurrence—he had not had any

accomplice except the Laird. He had, however, purposely endeavoured to raise an ill-feeling between Falcon and the crew, so that the new hand might bear the brunt of any suspicion that might be entertained as to the cause of the fire.

This information was derived from the Laird's statement. The Highlander himself continued obstinately silent, even after he had learned that the Laird, before he died, had told everything.

With the stolid placidity which characterized him he listened to the proceedings at his trial. When the jury had given their verdict, "Guilty," and the judge asked him if he had anything to say why sentence of death should not be pronounced, he answered—

"What would I'll say when you'll no change your minds? Shust gie us some ouskie, for it's tam dry wark hearkening to all this spoke about her own self."

Undisturbed he heard the doom spoken. Nothing could be got out of him except repeated demands for whisky.

"Oich but it was a bad day we'll saw Portlappoch again," he muttered on the morning
fixed for his execution; "but we'll see her no
more—Pe-tam."

As stolidly as if he had been ascending the
companion-way of his own vessel he ascended
the scaffold, and without a word of confession
or complaint submitted to his fate.

Donald, surly and discontented with everything and everybody, was set free after he
had given evidence at the trial. The crowd
hooted him—why, it would be difficult to
say, unless it might be that the crowd, which
is always more or less sentimental and hates
ingratitude even amongst rogues, fancied that
Donald merited contempt for bearing witness
against one who had been his friend. He
never appeared in Portlappoch again.

For several days after Wattie's funeral
Girzie had not been seen by any one save
Falcon. When at last she crossed the threshold of her own door to mingle again amongst
the toilers for bread, she was a bent broken-

down old woman, going about her work in a slow listless manner, never haggling now in buying or selling her fish. She displayed no concern for anything except the cuddy Dawnie. She treated the animal as if it had been human; and permitted it to grow fat and lazy without ever attempting to quicken it with the whip, which in former days she had used freely.

When Falcon became formally acknowledged as James Sutherland, and proprietor of Clashgirn, he offered her the means of living without the necessity of work.

"No," she answered, shaking her head drearily; "for the wee while I'm to be here, I maun dae something. When my hands are busy, they keep my head frae thinking. I maun daunner about wi' Dawnie alang the auld roads we used to travel when Wattie was wi' us; and it's a comfort to me whiles to fancy he's beside us yet at some weel-ken'd spot. I hear him and see him syne, and ken that I'll be wi' him again afore lang."

She never referred to the Laird or Carrach.

The only interest she displayed in their fate was by a slight start when she learned that the Laird was dead. A gleam of satisfaction flashed across her face as she said—

"I'm glad o' that."

Then she became silent and indifferent as before. She was obliged to appear as a witness at the trial of her brother; but no information was obtained from her beyond a repetition of her evidence as to the manner in which she had identified the body of her son. Several years afterward, however, she told the master of Clashgirn, then Captain Sutherland, why she had warned him not to sail in the *Colin.* She had overheard part of a conversation between the Laird and Carrach; and a careless observation the latter had made, when he had called on her before going on board, about the brig never coming to port again had roused her suspicions of meditated disaster. She had not made this known, because she had not wished to harm her brother or the Laird.

*　　*　　*　　*　　*

A clear cold morning, with a fresh breeze blowing in from the sea; the bright blue waves tossing foamily; the surge kissing the beach, and running away again with a loud song of invitation; and the fishing-boats, with sails spread, dancing on the water.

Gruff Adam Lindsay stood at the door of his cottage, his hand grasped by that of James Sutherland, whose face was slightly averted from the old man's dry unsympathetic gaze.

Hutcheson sat on the dyke hard by, swinging his legs, and staring at the two men, apparently interested in their conversation, but not minding much whether he heard it or not, being already aware of its purport.

"No, ye needna waken her," Sutherland was saying huskily; "I wasna meaning to see her at any rate. It's better for me maybe that I should not. But tell her that I was here; tell her that I'm going away for many years maybe; for I will never come back until I can take her hand with no other thought or feeling in my heart than what her friend and her guidman's should hae.

Good bye, Adam; I hope ye'll be alive and weel when I come hame again."

"I'll do your bidding wi' respect o' your message to my dochter. Good bye, sir, and a pleasant voyage," rejoined Adam, in much the same tone as if his friend had been about to make a trip to the Mull and back, instead of a journey round the world.

Sutherland shook the fisherman's hand warmly, and walked away at a rapid pace, as if afraid that he might be tempted to forego his resolution and seek an interview with Jeanie yet, which would only trouble her and himself too.

Hutcheson jumped off the dyke, and with a nod to Adam followed his some-time comrade.

"Ye're in an unco hurry to win awa'," he said, making up to him with a short race.

"Aye, I'm in a hurry," retorted Sutherland gloomily; "what should I bide for?"

"Naething particular that I ken o', except that it's a daft-like thing to rin awa' frae ane's fortune the minute ye get haud o't."

"Carnegie will take care of the fortune, as you call it, and Mrs. Begg will take care of the house. They could not be in better hands."

"Every ane to his ain gate, as the sang says. If it had been me, I would hae thought they would hae been better in my ain hands."

"You'll have enough in yours with the schooner."

Hutcheson's face brightened.

"Aye, that's true; the schooner's my fortune. It's the chance I hae been striving for this wheen years; and I hope there may be a time yet when I'll be able to satisfy ye that gieing ye the siller back is the least part o' the payment.

"I'm satisfied of that now. So take me to Southampton, and then make your fortune if you can."

The schooner *Ailsa* sailed that afternoon from Portlappoch, fully manned, Hutcheson occupying the position of skipper and owner, and James Sutherland that of a passenger.

Mr. Monduff and writer Carnegie went on
board to bid good-bye to the new laird of
Clashgirn before he set out on the journey,
which promised to be a long one. Both had
tried all their powers of persuasion to obtain
from him a promise of speedy return; but
they had failed.

"I have no wish," he said, with quiet firmness, "to neglect any of the duties which
belong to my altered circumstances; but,
honestly, I do not feel myself in a condition
to discharge them. Above all, I feel that it
is necessary to the peace of mind of others as
well as of myself that I should be away from
the Port for awhile. So, let us say no more
on that head now. When I come back, you
will perhaps acknowledge the advantages of
the course I am adopting, however weak it
may seem to you at present."

The minister grasped his hand.

"I believe you are right, Mr. Sutherland;
it is the course of a brave man to turn his
back on the disappointments of the past, and
to face the emergencies of the present with

a steady eye, and an earnest faith in the Lord's mercy. You will come back to us, I am sure, a contented, and therefore a happy man."

"I hope so, sir; thank you," was Sutherland's response, grateful for this sympathy. "I know that I may ask you to do something for me?"

"Of course—anything."

"Well, will you deliver this an hour after we have sailed?"

Mr. Monduff looked at the superscription of the letter which was placed in his hand, and appeared to hesitate.

"I spent the last hour or so writing it in the cabin," Sutherland said steadily, although his under lip quivered slightly; "and I have had my doubts about sending it, as you have yours about delivering it. But, trust me, sir, there is nothing in it which you might not read—or her guidman either"—(the latter words spoken with an effort).

"I'll do your bidding," said the minister, satisfied, and putting the letter in his pocket.

At length the tide had reached its height. Mr. Monduff and Carnegie stepped ashore at the last minute. The anchor was raised, and with a hearty cheer the *Ailsa* put off on her voyage.

CHAPTER XVI.

JAMES SUTHERLAND TO MRS. GRAY.

> " The soldier frae the war returns,
>   And the merchant frae the main;
> But I hae parted wi' my love,
>   And ne'er to meet again."—*Cavalier Song.*

" I am almost afraid to write; and yet the desire, or the temptation—or whatever the feeling may be called—is so strong upon me, that to relieve myself from a condition of nervous irritability I am compelled to sit down here and talk to you by the means of this paper. Whether you shall ever see it or not is a question to be decided afterwards.

"This is written in the cabin of the *Ailsa* —the place you were locked up in by Carrach. I am going to join my ship at Southampton; and we sail as soon as the tide rises. Hard work, time, and absence will help me to get over the ——

"I stopped there; and for the last ten minutes I have been chewing the end of my pen because I did not know what word might be written in that place without offence to the wife of another man, and yet be true to my own feelings. Suppose we call it weakness, for it must be weakness that, in spite of my desire and resolution to the contrary, makes me think so much about you. One queer character of my thoughts puzzles me: they always fix upon you as you were on that afternoon before the *Colin* sailed, when we parted at the door of the cottage. I address you as Mrs. Gray; and if you were beside me now I would speak to you by that name; but I cannot *think* of you so.

"I have tried it—tried hard; but just when I seem to be catching a glimpse of you standing by his side as his wife, everything seems to fade from me except the memory of that hour when we parted with eyes looking hopefully to our meeting. Don't be angry with me for minding you of that. I did not mean to do it; but I seem to be writing in a

kind of a daze, scarcely knowing what words
my pen forms until they are down. I want
to let you see my thought; I want to let you
see my heart—not that you may be distressed
by the sight of its sadness, but that you may
be comforted, if you need comfort, by the
knowledge of my determination to submit to
the fate that has befallen us, and to conquer
the weakness—aye, it is weakness, and bitter,
bitter to thole—the weakness that unfits me
for the duties of a man, and one whom
Heaven has been kind to for all the grief
that I have suffered. You see I speak of it
already as of a thing gone by; and that is
some gain.

"I wanted to see you before I left; and
yet I wanted to spare you and myself the
pain of another meeting. That is the thraw-
ard state my mind has been in ever since
we were brought together again on board this
boat—ever since you cried to me to come
and help you. I am glad that I was able to
do what I have done; but I am gladdest of all
to remember that I have been able to take

Robin Gray's hand in friendship over the grave of poor Wattie Todd, whose death, under the direction of Him who leads us through darkness into light, became the instrument of restoring your peace and your guidman's.

"It was at Wattie's grave that I felt the first glow of real strength. What my duty was I had recognized a while before; but it had been in bitterness and with girning heart, that made me conscious of how little power I had to fulfil the duty. There seemed to be only one chance of doing it, and that was by running away, by putting miles of land and water between you and me. But at Wattie's grave I became conscious that it was a coward's view I was taking of the case; that it was a mean snivelling sort of fear which made me believe I could never be honest if I allowed myself to be near you to see you and hear your voice.

"Then I discovered for the first time that my duty was to bow my head in submission to the will that had directed our lives other-

wise than as we had planned them. I learned
that the conduct of a true man was to regard
your position with sacred respect; and to
overcome the pitiful chagrin which rendered
me incapable of looking calmly on your happiness and Cairnieford's, much less of taking
pleasure in it.

"From that minute I turned with steady
purpose to learn such respect for you, and to
overcome that miserable envy—for it was
nothing better—which made me look on
Robin Gray unkindly. So much is not to
be acquired in a day, or a week maybe; but
with God's help I will acquire it, and if I
ever come back to Portlappoch it will be
with heart and mind purified of all useless
regrets, and able to sympathize in the joys of
your home.

"This was what I wanted to tell you when
I went up to the cottage in the morning. I
wanted to satisfy you that I was not going
away the despairing wretched man you parted
from at Askaig; but one who having made
shipwreck of certain old hopes and dreams,

had turned stoutly to seek new hopes and new aims in the busiest scenes of the world's strife.

"I wanted to tell you all about that; but when I got near to the house I felt something like the old weakness coming over me; and I feared that in spite of my resolution I would become a coward in your presence; and that the cruel thoughts which troubled me when first I was made aware how fate had separated us would rise anew, leaving me unworthy of a good woman's memory.

"I was almost glad when your father told me that you were sleeping; and yet I was sorry too. But I minded of Wattie Todd, and that helped the wiser part of me to get the upper hand. So I bade Adam not to waken you. I gave him a message for you, and came away thankful that I had made at least one step in the right direction in leaving without disturbing you.

"It is better so for both of us. I know that; and yet I have been tortured and haunted all day by the notion that it would have been manlier for me to have said to you with my own lips what I have said here. The notion has followed me about, so that I have not been able to do anything, or to feel at ease, until I sat down to write this. I think there is nothing here that ought not to have been said; nothing that you need be ashamed to read or I to send.

"I only want you to be happy—aye, and now I can say sincerely that I wish Robin Gray to live long to share that happiness with you. Having helped him for your sake seems to have done me good, and I am grateful to both of you for it. I am grateful to him besides for the help which I know now he wished to give me when he thought I needed it. That said, I already feel stronger and better in myself.

"In the madness which beset me when I first learned that the object upon which I had bent my life was placed beyond my reach, I fancied there never could be any light in this world for me. Sitting here with the tide rising to carry me away to where strong hands are needed—with the water beating against the vessel and rocking me like a bairn in a cradle—I can review quietly all that is past, and feel that there is a future of honourable work for me that will bring pleasure with it, and of blessed content for you and yours.

"When I come back I will expect you to give me a welcome home; and I will expect your bairns and your man to join in the welcome.

"Be kind to Girzie Todd, for she suffers more than any of us by what has happened. Good bye, and Heaven bless and prosper you and your husband,

Your faithful servant,

JAMES SUTHERLAND."

Mr. Monduff was seated by the bedside whilst Jeanie slowly read the letter which he had delivered. He watched her with a paternal interest, waiting patiently until she had read it a second time, pausing at certain passages as if to 'fix their meaning on her memory.

Her eyes brightened and her face flushed. She was pleased by the generous nature of the writer which was revealed in every line: how nobly he tried to conceal his own pain that he might lighten hers; how bravely he set himself to do whatever work might be assigned him, and to thrust aside all vain and selfish repining for the disappointment he had endured.

She was glad he had written; she was glad he had enabled her to understand the healthy frame of mind with which he started on his voyage. She was proud to have been loved by such a man; proud, without one thought which an angel could have blamed as an injustice to Robin Gray. The truth and courage which were revealed in this letter strengthened her in proportion to the relief she experienced on the writer's account. It made her a happier woman, and a better wife, in directing her eyes to the light in the future, than she ever could have been had she been haunted by the recollection of the grief which she had caused him. The letter seemed to have brought sunlight into the sick chamber.

"You are gratified by what he says," observed the minister, a little curious.

"Read it, sir," she answered, placing the letter in his hand.

Mr. Monduff obeyed, and his face also brightened as he read; for his attachment to the writer made him sincerely anxious about his welfare.

"This is capital," he said warmly; "when a man has made up his mind to have a bad tooth out, the toothache is half-cured. That's just his case; and you will see him come home, marry some worthy woman, and settle down in a happy and respected home. Keep the letter, Mistress Gray, and show it to Cairnieford as soon as you can. It will do him as much good to read it as it has done me. The plans which James Falcon formed have miscarried, as he says; but they have opened a path to a noble life of usefulness and goodness."

"I believe that, sir, and I ken that he will follow it wi' steady steps and a brave heart."

"And you will do the same, I hope, Mistress Gray?"

"I'll try, sir."

"Then you will begin at once by sending for your guidman, and telling him that you have forgiven the misunderstanding of which he was as much the victim as yourself. Shall I bring him to-day?"

"Dinna ask me to do that yet, sir," she said imploringly; "I canna do it. It's no because there is ony anger in my heart against him; but I canna feel sure o' him being as free frae doubt o' me as he maun be before I can take my place in his house again."

"It is you who doubt him now"—(gently reproachful).

"I canna explain mysel' very weel. I ken his kind nature, grieving ower what has happened, makes him anxious to mend the break atween us; but I'm feared, feared that after a while, or when ony bit quarrel got the better o' us, he might be sorry that we had

cam' thegither again. But I dinna understand my ain feelings, sir, in the matter;
whiles I'm like to greet thinking o' him, and
syne I feel that it would be wrang o' me to
gie in to the first offer that his gratitude wins
frae him. Ye'll call that pride and vanity
maybe, and nae doubt ye would be right, sir;
though I dinna feel it that way. Gie me
time to think—dinna press me enow."

The minister felt that he ought to have
reprimanded this stubbornness and inconsis-
tency of the woman's nature; but she spoke
with such simple earnestness that he could
not find it in his heart to show even displea-
sure. So:—

"Ah, well, we will give you time," he said
quietly; "and the more readily as I have great
faith in that remedy. But remember, you
are on the wrong side now."

"I'm sorry for that, sir, for I canna do
what ye want. Even if he didna think sae,
I would feel that it was like taking advantage
o' his position, and I couldna thole that. I
gaed to him when he was in the hands o' the

fiscal, and he wasna ower weel pleased to see me, as I hae mentioned to ye. I told him then that when the work was done and he was safe, I wouldna fash him ony mair. I canna bring mysel' yet to take back the words. Ye'll no blame me ower muckle, sir? I would like to do onything that is right; but I canna feel that it would be right to profit by his gratitude. It would be like making a bargain out o' what has been done."

"You'll see it in another light soon, Mistress Gray," was the minister's answer.

Jeanie wished to see it in another light. She even owned to herself that her conduct was perverse and obstinate; that she was permitting pride to stand between her and the reconciliation which she knew ought to be made for her own sake and others. But whenever she thought of telling her father to bring Robin into the house, the memory of his coldness to her on that day of the fiscal's examination restrained her kindly impulse.

She heard very little of his doings, for

Adam would not mention his name. Bessie
Tait, however, was able to give her a little
information, which she obtained from one of
the servants at the farm. Bessie was acting
as nurse, and quickly discovering that Jeanie
liked to hear about Cairnieford, she gathered
all the news about him that came within her
hearing and carefully retailed it to her friend.

Jeanie listened and reflected. The new
light was beginning to penetrate the sick
chamber; and that letter the minister had
delivered had some share in clearing the
darkness. The whole trouble became little
more than a question as to which should yield
first: and it would soon have been settled
if Robin had only known the real state of
Jeanie's mind.

CHAPTER XVII.

ROBIN'S GRACE.

"The oak that all winter was barren and bare,
  Again spreads his branches to wave in the air;
  All nature, rejoicing, appears clad in green."—*Anon.*

But Robin did not know, and he was pro-
foundly unhappy in consequence. He took
all the blame to himself, and he went about
the farm with a fidgety irritable manner that
puzzled everybody who had dealings with
him. He could not settle to do anything;
and he kept moving about from place to
place as if the spirit of unrest had taken possession of him, and doomed him to a state of
continual motion.

Since the day of his release, he had not
visited the town more than half a dozen
times, although he was at Adam's cottage
every morning. But on the second market-
day after the sailing of the *Ailsa*, he dressed

himself, and proceeded to the Port, as had
been his custom on these occasions for many
years. He had no cattle or grain to sell or
buy; he had no business of the ordinary
kind to transact, and he did not care much
about the market itself now. He had lost
interest in almost all those objects which
formerly occupied him, and he was indifferent
as to whether the price of grain were up or
down. But for all that, he had a definite
purpose in attending the market. He was
driven to it chiefly by the spirit of unrest
that was upon him, and partly by his desire
to learn how recent events had affected him
in the regard of his old friends. He had
been in jail; the suspicion of crime had been
attached to him; and he wanted to show his
acquaintances and the folk generally that he
could take his former place amongst them,
and hold his head erect with conscious innocence.

He expected that many would shrink from
him; that he would be received with cold
looks and colder greetings; and that all would

treat him as one who had lost his right to
the position of an unblemished man. But he
was mistaken; he was received with hearty
congratulations by every one. There was
not the faintest expression of blame on any
of the ruddy countenances which pressed
around him; there was not the faintest hint
of doubt as to his honesty pronounced by
any of the tongues which welcomed him back
to his old place: all hands were eager to
grasp his, and all eyes brightened at sight of
him.

He was confounded a little at first by so
much good humour; but presently he began
to experience a sense of relief, which would
have rendered him perfectly happy had he
not remembered that the one whose smile
was worth more than all the kindness of the
others had not welcomed him yet, and that
Cairnieford was desolate in consequence. That
thought stung him to the quick, and made
him appear somewhat moody in the midst of
the good-will with which he was received.
He had gone there with dogged resolution to

carry his head proudly in the teeth of the scorn and sneering looks which he had expected to encounter; but nobody scorned him, and nobody sneered at him; and so the motive for his resolution failing him, he was driven back upon the one source of discontent.

He was, however, obliged to drink many drams to his own prosperity; and what with the drams, the congratulations, and the jokes, he became somewhat gleeful towards evening, and was rather late in quitting the Port Inn. Stepping away from the door, he stumbled against young Dunbar.

"Hallo, Jock," he cried, slapping him on the shoulder, "ye're late in the town. Are ye gaun hame?"

"No yet, Cairnie," answered Dunbar, a little awkwardly, and trying to laugh.

"No! Weel, I thought we might hae gaen thegither sae far. But what are ye biding for?"

"A friend I want to see particularly," was the response, whilst he became more awkward than before, and attempted to get away. "I hae been waiting three hours for her—for him I mean——"

"Oh, ho, I see what's in the wind!" cried Cairnieford, giving him another hearty slap on the shoulder, and laughing. "Never be ashamed o't. If she's a guid thrifty lass, marry her, and I'll dance the bauchles aff my feet at your weddin'."

"Thank ye, Cairnie," said Dunbar, joining in the laugh, and recovering his self-possession now the truth was out; "ye'll maybe hae the chance sooner than ye think."

"I'm glad to hear't, lad. I gie ye joy; but wha's the lass? Do I ken her?"

"Ye do that, for it's just Bessie Tait wha was bridesmaid at yer ain weddin'."

"Eh, is it her?" She's a braw lass, and will make a sonsy wife, I doubtna. But mind, Jock, and ay keep the right side o' bad speaking. Thrapple the first man that says an ill word against her."

"See if I dinna"—(with enthusiastic resolution).

" Where is she the noo?"

"She's just waiting on your guidwife, and hasna got hame yet."

" Waiting on Jeanie?—what a gowk I was no to think o' that afore. Jock, I maun see your lass—dinna be feared, man, I'll no spoil sport. But I maun speak twa or three words wi' her, and syne I'll leave her to yoursel'."

He saw her and spoke a good many more than three words to her. He had so many things to ask, and so many things to say, about Jeanie, that Dunbar became impatient, and slyly asked if he would come back in the morning, by which time perhaps Robin would have finished.

Cairnieford took the hint. He was a happier man than he had been for many days, for he had learned that Jeanie was not only as well as could be expected, but spoke of him often, always asking Bessie if she had heard how he was getting on. From which fact Bessie naively argued that Jeanie did not altogether hate her guidman.

A cunning plot was entered upon by these

dark conspirators, and Bessie was to be the prime agent of its progress. When that was agreed upon, Dunbar was relieved by Robin's departure, his nose sniffing the keen night air with the greatest enjoyment, and his feet touching the ground with the lightness of youth.

He set to work now with a will. Mackie, the grieve, was astonished next morning to find him going about with all his old interest in the affairs of the farm. His manner was still restless; but there was a strong undercurrent of hope which cleared away the nervous anxiety that had made him so fidgety and so unsettled in all he had attempted to do, or had directed to be done, since he had come home. He was now setting everything in order, and he became especially attentive to the arrangements inside the house.

"That's a guid sign," observed Mackie to the lass who told him about this; "we'll hae the mistress hame sune, or I'm mista'en."

As matters were progressing, it looked exceedingly probable that the grieve would not be mistaken.

Every day Robin saw Bessie Tait, and obtained from her fuller and more satisfactory reports as to Jeanie's condition than he could wring from the grim and unforgiving Adam.

He saw the old man every morning as usual, however, but he failed to make any impression on his stern nature that might tend to soften his memory of what had occurred at Girzie Todd's place.

When the spring came with its green leaves and bright hearty days, a baby was born in fisher Lindsay's cottage. Then said Robin:—

"I will see my bairn—I will see my wife. I hae waited lang enuch; I will wait nae langer."

So he went to the cottage, and Bessie Tait, who had been watching for his coming, ran to the door and admitted him before Adam could say a word.

Then she placed the bairn—a sturdy boy
with big blue eyes—in his arms. He took
the little thing as awkwardly as if it had
been a figure of glass, and he had been afraid
to break it.

"And it's a laddie tae—aye, aye!" he cried,
looking at it with open-mouthed wonder.

At this juncture the little fellow began to
cry with a vigour which was most satisfactory, as indicative of healthy lungs, and
Bessie would have taken it from him. But:

"Na, na," said Robin, "I'll haud the bonnie
wee dollie—puir wee man," and in a clumsy
way he began to dandle it, and to cry "hush
—sh—sh!"

Then kindly Bessie enticed grim Adam out
of the room, and closed the door.

Jeanie did not speak although her eyes and
heart were full of tears, and a quiet joy made
the blood dance through her veins, so that
she felt as if that moment atoned for all that
she had suffered.

Robin felt awkward; burning to speak, and
yet not knowing how to begin. So he rocked

the little one in his arms, and cried "whist ye, whist ye, my bonnie lamb;" and uttered a series of extraordinary sounds which he supposed to be baby language, but the source and the meaning of which he could not have explained for the life of him. He tried to laugh whilst uttering the gibberish, and all the time the big brawny fellow's eyes were, like the mother's, glistening with tears of pleasure and hope.

At last he looked at the mother, whose pale face was turned towards him.

"Jeanie," he cried, with the baby singing a chorus, "will naething move ye to forgie me —winna our bairn do't?"

And he held the child in his outstretched arms, as if to let it plead for him. She took the bairn to her breast, hushing its cries, and then she answered with a low tender voice:

"I hae done that lang syne, Robin; for I ken ye maun hae tholed muckle sorrow. But——"

"Dinna say but," he cried, bending over her; "God kens what I hae tholed; and God kens that it was because ye were sae dear to me that I was sae blind."

"You're e'en are open noo?"

"Aye; but what guid is that to me, if they are only open to let me see what I hae lost, to let me see that there is nae hope for me o' winning it back in this world? Dinna send me awa', Jeanie; for the bairn's sake dinna send me awa'."

She looked straight in his eyes.

" Ye hae nae doubt left in your heart that I hae told you the truth?"

" Ye mind me o' my ain shame—ye mind me that I wish the tongue had been cut frae my mouth afore it had spoken the words it did; ye mind me o' my ain misery when ye speir that."

"But it might rise atween us again; and that is what gar'd me think it would be better for us no to be thegither ony mair."

" Ye winna trust me "—(bitterly). "O woman, if there could be onything come atween you and me again, the mindin' o' that night at Askaig would make me crush it aneath my foot like the pooshen head o' a serpent."

A pause, she gazing earnestly in his face. Then, satisfied:

"I believe ye, Robin."

"And ye'll come hame?"

Another pause; then, very softly:

"For the bairn's sake and your's as weel— yes."

"God be thanked."

He stooped down, and kissed her.

And so the bairn came, as the fable has it, with an angel's message; and this particular message was one of grace to Robin Gray.

CHAPTER XVIII.

A POSTSCRIPT.

"Time and tide had thus their sway,
Yielding, like an April day,
Smiling noon for sullen morrow,
Years of joy for hours of sorrow."—*Scott.*

Mr. Carnegie rubbed his hands with satisfaction; the minister smiled, and the minister's wife shared her husband's content. They were seated in the parlour of the manse; and the subject of conversation was the reconciliation of the Master and Mistress of Cairnieford.

"There is nobody more pleased wi' the upshot o' the habble than I am," observed the lawyer; "and as things have come about it is as well that our young laird is left a bachelor; for now he may seek a wife of education and position. If it was not for that I would be almost sorry that he had not

got the lass he had so set his mind on. She
would have been a lucky woman if she had
only waited a wee."

"I think she is a lucky woman as it is,"
commented the minister; "we may regret
that they have both had to suffer so much;
but it is their sacrifice, as we may call it,
which has proved their worth. She is a
nobler woman, and he a nobler man, in having
loved and parted as they have done, than
they ever could have been, had any dispen-
sation removed Robin Gray, and permitted
them to become united. That might have
contented them; but it could never have had
half the value in the happiness of their lives
that they will find in the consciousness of
their fidelity to honour."

"Just so, sir, just so; but suppose it had
been possible for Cairnieford to stand aside—"

"But you cannot suppose that, since he
became her husband; and that sacred barrier
once raised, it is impious to wish or to attempt
to break it down. No, no, the life that lies
before Mistress Gray and James Sutherland,

is, in view of all the circumstances, the truest and best."

"That may be—indeed I have no doubt that it is as you say," continued the lawyer, who did not like to yield an argument even to the minister; "but Sutherland will never be the happy man he might have been had he been spared this disappointment."

"Hoot toot, Carnegie, you would fill the world wi' misanthropes. Man, our capabilities of enjoyment are mercifully unlimited. There never was a wound—mind, I make a distinction between wound and disease— there never was a wound, moral or physical, that time could not heal. We part from old friends and old associations, and we feel a sting at the off-going. But in a wee while we form new friendships and new associations, and are just as contented wi' them as we ever were wi' the old ones. You're no sentimental, are ye?"

"I hope no!" exclaimed Carnegie, horrified at the suggestion of such a weakness in a lawyer.

"Ah, weel, then, you'll have to admit the truth o' what I have said."

The minister's wife so evidently sided with the minister that, to save his reputation as a responsible law-agent, Carnegie was obliged to yield.

Jeanie and the bairn were removed to Cairnieford as speedily after the re-union as circumstances permitted. In a little while she was bustling about the house, happy and contented. Robin's joy in his wife and child was as perfect as mortal's joy ever can be.

Dame Lindsay lived to enjoy many pleasant days in the bright home up the glen; and when her time came she passed peacefully away in her daughter's arms. Adam gave a silent acquiescence to the new arrangements; but no argument or prayer could prevail on him to quit the cottage—which he now occupied rent-free by the instructions of the young laird—to take up his abode at Cairnieford. He taught the bairns, as they grew up, to fish and row, to mend nets, to

make boats and sail them; but he never overcame a certain degree of stiffness in all his
dealings with Robin.

When, years after his departure in the
Ailsa, Captain Sutherland came home, one of
the first places he visited was Cairnieford.
Half-a-dozen children ran out to greet him,
the guidman grasped his hand in hearty welcome, and the guidwife received him with a
happy matronly smile. The minister's words
were verified, and memory cast no shade on
the meeting. There was no twinge of regret
or envy in his heart when he saw the content which made the farmer's home bright.
He could share their pleasures as a faithful
friend; he could romp with the bairns; and
he was as proud as a father might have been
of the little fellow to whom his name had
been given.

He was neither a crabbed nor a misanthro-
pical man; but frank and jovial, with lively
sympathies for all that was good and true.
And he soon disclosed his admiration for the
embodiment of these qualities; for one day

it became known that Captain Sutherland was about to be married. The minister regarded the fact as another proof of the temporary nature of human despair. At any rate the Captain found a worthy mistress for his house; and the memory of his old passion, on the rare occasions when it recurred to him, was greeted with a quiet smile in which there was no sadness.

THE END.

GLASGOW: W. G. BLACKIE AND CO., PRINTERS, VILLAFIELD.

www.ingramcontent.com/pod-product-compliance
Lightning Source LLC
Chambersburg PA
CBHW021040030726
47496CB00006B/1622